OCT 2 3 '95			
NOV 1 6 '9			
NOV 2 8 '99			
MAY 2 9 '9			
MAR 0 2 '99			
AUG 1 2 '99			

RIC

BETRAYAL IN TOMBSTONE

Katie Elder had a reputation that stretched from Wichita to California. She was the Queen of the Bargirls—but no man could claim her until Doc Holliday came around. Holliday was a legend all his own—gambler, killer, sometime doctor, and the outlaw partner of Wyatt Earp. Doc said he'd never met a woman he'd kill for—but that was before he met Big Nose Kate. From Dodge City to Tombstone they gambled and fought and ran from the law. They were the West's most legendary lovers—until the day she betrayed him. Now Doc was looking for Kate—with murder on his mind.

BETRAYAL IN TOMBSTONE

RAY HOGAN

WESTERNS

First published 1975 by the Popular Library

This hardback edition 1995
by Chivers Press
by arrangement with
the Golden West Literary Agency

ISBN 0 7451 4634 1

British Library Cataloguing in Publication Data available

Printed and bound in Great Britain by
Redwood Books, Trowbridge, Wiltshire

BETRAYAL IN TOMBSTONE

1

"That," John Shanssey said in reply to the question Big Nose Kate had put to him, "is Doc Holliday."

They were standing in front of his saloon, a sprawling, barnlike affair on Griffin Street in the booming Texas settlement called The Flat. In the warm afternoon haze that lay upon the land all things seemed to be in erratic motion—horses, vehicles, the assortment of cowhands, buffalo hunters, soldiers, drummers, merchants, even a few of the ordinarily indolent Tonkawa Indians who were camped outside nearby Fort Griffin.

Doc Holliday, the gambler—the killer. Kate studied the man who had just alighted from the southbound stage and now stood in the loose dust of the street, dust that would become thick, knee-deep, clinging mud during the rainy season. He looked like a dude but she knew to believe so could be fatal. The most dangerous man in the country, she'd heard him called by those who should know, and seeing him for the first time set her spine to tingling.

5

There was a distinct aura to him, a mantle of threat, of violence coolly promised that could not be missed. Blond, an inch or two short of six feet in height, he'd probably weigh about a hundred and sixty, Kate reckoned, sizing him up deliberately. He appeared lean and sinewy in the soft brown suit, flat-heeled boots, white shirt with a black string tie and medium brimmed hat.

His features seemed to be chiseled rather than formed. The corners of his face were square and definite, while the skin stretched tight across the bones had a sort of translucence. He was a dying man—consumption she thought it was, and that was probably what gave his blue-gray eyes a sort of luminous brilliance. A sweeping, leonine mustache graced his upper lip and partly hid the sardonic smile with which he was viewing The Flat.

"What's bringing him here?" Kate wondered. "Dump like this—"

"Doc goes where the money is. Right now that's here."

"Could do better'n this."

Shanssey glanced over his shoulder into the smoky, lamplit depths of what he preferred to call his casino. Within its thin walls he catered to man's every whim—drink, dance, gambling, women—anything a customer wanted, and business was better than just good. He could barely see inside the murky room but the steady din issuing from it was a satisfying sound.

"It's not the fancy-looking places a man like Doc Holliday goes for. It's how much money's around that counts."

Holliday had not moved. He simply stood at the edge of the street in front of the hotel, his steel-hard, bright gaze drifting over the ragtag structures and the restless crowd that made up the town. Reaching into an inside pocket, he drew forth a handkerchief and coughed into it.

"He a real doctor or is that just what they call him?" Kate wondered.

Shanssey shrugged. "Reckon he's the genuine article, all right. Don't know what kind."

Her brows lifted. "A real doctor, eh?" she murmured. "What the hell's he doing wasting his time gambling?"

"Maybe he makes more money at it," Shanssey said and turned to re-enter the saloon. "Got to be getting back to work. You coming?"

Kate nodded. "In a minute."

The saloonman paused in the doorway, cast a critical eye at her. "If you're thinking of shining up to Doc Holliday you'd best watch your step."

"Why? All the stories I've heard about him and women don't scare me none. Expect I could teach him a trick or two, was I of the mind."

"Expect you could," Shanssey agreed, "but I wasn't meaning that."

Puzzled, Kate frowned at him. "Then what—"

"Been said he'd as lief kill a man as not. Knows he ain't going to be around for long, what with the bugs about to get him, so he plain don't give a good goddamn about himself. A man facing that's afraid of nothing 'cause he knows he's the same as dead anyway."

"Still don't see why you're telling me all this," Kate said. "I'm not going to push him into drawing his pistol on me—though it might be good for some laughs. You know if he ever shot a woman, John?"

7

"Probably has, so I wouldn't go getting any ideas about throwing down on him with that gun you're carrying, if I was you. He won't take it as a joke."

Kate smiled, fingered the derringer in the pocket of the dress she was wearing. Two men brushed by her, nodding and smiling. She winked at both, then put her attention back on Holliday, enduring another coughing spell.

"Like as not you're right. He don't seem much the kind you could do any funning with, but you just never know from looking."

"Well, if ever you take the notion to find out, be sure you got yourself a place in the graveyard picked out," Shanssey said dryly, and continued on into the saloon.

Kate continued to watch Holliday. Something about him fascinated her. Shortly he had evidently completed his broad, surface examination of the town and made up his mind as to whatever points had been in question. Now, carpetbag in his left hand, he turned about and considered the weathered façade of the hotel.

Somewhere down the street a burst of gunshots broke out and she saw him swing his sharp, pallid features in that direction. Men, attracted by the shooting, began to quicken their steps and hurry toward the point where a crowd was hastily gathering. Gunshots, despite the fact they were common enough in The Flat, still drew considerable attention, with interest centering primarily on who the victim was, and secondarily, on who had pulled the trigger.

It was Jake Ackerman's saloon, Kate realized, making out the sign on the false front of the structure through freshly stirred clouds of dust. Probably a couple of buffalo hunters settling an argument. They preferred Jake's place because the rotgut he served was cheaper—and that suited Kate fine since it kept them out of Shanssey's; all buffalo hunters apparently had sworn a blood oath never to bathe.

She saw Holliday brush the tail of his coat aside, caught a glimpse of the pistol he wore on his right leg—a nickel-plated weapon in a Mexican-style holster. A man always ready and expecting trouble, he did it unconsciously, she guessed.

The town marshal and his young deputy hurried by, their faces set in anticipation, paying no heed to questions shouted at them or to Holliday, who continued to stare fixedly at the still-growing crowd in front of Ackerman's.

The blond hair pushing out from beneath his flat crowned hat was thick and neatly trimmed, Kate noted, and that part of his neck visible between its edge and his collar was pink as if he'd just been shaved. He was a man seldom out in the open under the sun, that was certain. But that was to be expected. Gamblers pursuing their profession knew only the late afternoon's light and that for only a brief time.

Their day began somewhere between noon and dark, generally around midway, and ended with dawn, whereupon their night and the hours for sleep were at hand. Such was the usual schedule; in the occasional games that lasted for days and nights, no note was taken whether it was dark or daylight and time was neither noticed nor known. Considering his affliction, Doc Holliday had chosen the worst possible way to use up the remainder of his life.

He had lost interest in the shooting. Onlookers, too, were turning away, heading back up Griffin

Street. A man in a buckboard whirled by, scattering pedestrians in all directions. Several of them took the moment to shower him with curses. Two soldiers who had been in conversation with one of the girls from Nosey Kate's house suddenly began to fight, swinging wildly at each other and drawing a second crowd.

Holliday, as if resigning himself to the inevitable, took a firm grip on his bag and, adjusting the angle of his hat, started toward the door of the hotel. Kate, a surge of customary recklessness abruptly pushing through her, came to a decision. Why not line up with the famous Doc Holliday, become his woman? It ought to be fun—and good for a lot of excitement.

"Hold it, sport!" she called brashly, and moved toward him.

2

Sighing, Holliday stepped down from the stage-coach. Dust was still spinning within its interior, where he had been the lone passenger for the past five hours. He was glad to plant his boots on solid ground again. Traveling wasn't the lark it once was, and the dry air and dust, despite copious quantities of whiskey, caused him to cough more—and deeper. Sometimes he thought he was going to heave up his lungs, but he guessed he'd just about done that already.

A half-smile plucked his thin lips as he thought back to the two women who had earlier left the coach at a settlement called Dindy. To alleviate a particularly bad spell which had seized him shortly before the stop, he had tipped the bottle for a prolonged swallow. The older of the pair had bristled like a terrier at the sight of a hedgehog.

"If you'd stop drinking that poison you wouldn't have that terrible cough!" she informed him huffily.

He had nodded and said: "Just as the egg preceded the chicken, madam, the cough came first."

11

Such had been the extent of conversation between the three passengers of the big coach as it popped and swayed along the Texas roadway, bearing south. A man who ordinarily kept to himself, a true loner in fact, he had found this journey unaccountably boring.

Thinking back on it, Doc smiled a somewhat bitter, cynical grimace. Womenfolk were forever after him to stop drinking, to take better care of himself on penalty of dying young. Well, he was twenty-five and to all purposes was a dead man right then. It was just a matter of winding up the final days, or months—certainly not many years—and then being planted in some boneyard somewhere with other misfits and castoffs of society. When and where that event took place was of no real import.

The Flat . . . He stood where he had stepped down from the coach, waited until it had whirled away, and then let his glance rake the collection of shacks and buildings that made up the settlement. It was no different from a hundred other boomtowns he had ridden into, tarried in for a while, and then forsaken.

The same squalid, hastily erected structures, the same desperately eager people in search of something; dust, heat, the stench of unwashed bodies, of drying buffalo hides, of smoke, whiskey, coal oil, rank perfume, and from somewhere, as if to relieve the mundane, the good, wholesome smell of freshly baked bread.

But with it all came also the cool feel of gold and silver coins, the softness of worn paper money, the pleasant snick of cards, and the whirr of the wheels. That was what made it all bearable—not so much the money itself, but the winning of it, those

12

moments of tension when the stakes were high and a man bet his judgment against that of others, and won. Then came that inner flush, that soothing glow of victory.

He had pursued that sensation from those first days in Dallas, where he had gone after a physician in Atlanta had told him he was a dying man with one or perhaps two years of life remaining, if he moved to a dry climate and took care of himself.

The former he did, the latter he left in the hands of chance. Dallas, a thriving metropolis of some three thousand souls at the time of his arrival in 1873, proved to offer a more lucrative way of life in the gambling halls than in his profession of dentistry and soon he was devoting most of his time to the cards. Success was cut short, however, when he had the misfortune of choosing too prominent an individual as a victim in a gunfight.

There had been others before who had foolishly dared to outshoot the drawling gambler-dentist from Georgia. They had failed but there had been no repercussions resulting from those engagements. The last was different, and in his own best interests Dr. John H. Holliday left town in a hurry.

After that came the Indian Territory for a cooling period, then back to Texas—but not Dallas—and the Colorado towns of Denver, Pueblo, Trinidad, Cheyenne in Wyoming, and now some five years later, The Flat, a settlement near Fort Griffin on a fork of the Brazos River.

There was plenty of money there, he'd been told. Buffalo hunters were cashing in big, soldiers were plentiful and easy plucking, if never very affluent. Drovers were to be found and accommodated in sea-

13

son and there was always a flow of pilgrims passing through who elected to lay over for a few days.

Saloons, gambling and dance halls, as a unit or separate, never closed and the supply of women—the major drawing card for the hunters, soldiers, and cowhands, as well as the local gentry—was boundless.

He'd get himself a room at the hotel, such as it appeared to be, clean up a bit and then make himself acquainted with John Shanssey, an ex-boxer turned saloonkeeper, who, he'd been advised, ran the best place in The Flat. When things began to cool off as they always did, he'd move on—assuming he didn't cash in during the meantime.

Turning, he started for the entrance to the hostelry, a ramshackle building only months old but already in the first stages of decay. There had to be something better, he was sure, and he'd look into it later. Right now he'd—

Gunshots down the street drew his attention. He half-turned, studied the focal point of a surging crowd in front of a saloon some distance farther on. One man was on his knees, head slumped forward as he clutched his belly. Blood was coloring his fingers. Nearby a tall, burly looking hide-hunter stood with a smoking pistol in his hand.

Voices were yelling and shortly two lawmen, their features set, hurried by. Holliday shrugged. You'd think people who lived in places like The Flat would get used to killings but they never seemed to, despite the fact that violence and death were merely factors in living. Maybe it was he—and men like him—who were always so near death that they could look at it from an objective standpoint; or it could be only he, a man dead but alive and awaiting only the final rites.

14

Smiling wryly at his thoughts, Holliday turned again to the hotel but halted as a woman's light tones coming from the front of a saloon a few steps up the street reached him.

"Hold it, sport—"

Amused, he swung about, gave her his attention as she swaggered toward him. Of medium height, she was well built with high, full breasts and smoothly curving hips. Her hair and eyes were a matching dark brown and her features, except for the nose, which was somewhat large, were attractive and regular.

She had an air of reckless independence, a definite sort of vitality that bespoke a will of her own, a strength to do anything she set her mind to, while still preserving a womanly softness. She was clad in a rose-colored dress that revealed the shape of her well-turned legs. The arch of her bosom and the pure physical attractiveness of her reached out to him and held his attention.

"Something on your mind, lady?" he asked in his rich Southern accent.

She made a flippant gesture toward the hotel. "Dump is a fleabag. If you've never got yourself acquainted with bedbugs and lice, you will in there."

Holliday glanced around. "There a better one?"

"No, they're all fleabags."

He smiled wanly. "Gives me no choice."

"There's my place."

He considered her with interest. "You wouldn't happen to be Nosey Kate, would you? Was told she ran a house here."

"No, I'm not," she replied flatly. "Name's Kate, all right. Folks I like sometimes call me Big Nose Kate, if I'm feeling good."

15

"My apologies. I'm Doc Hol—"

"Know who you are. Saw you get off the stage—Shanssey and me. He told me." She paused, ducked her head at the hotel. In the lowering sunlight her skin took on a softer glow where rice powder and rouge had been brushed away. "What about it? You staying in there or moving in with me?"

Holliday covered his mouth with a cupped hand and coughed. "Only a fool would refuse your offer," he said gallantly.

She gave him a wide smile, nodded. "Then let's go. Expect you'd like to get settled," she said crisply and turned toward a row of small cabins at the rear of Shanssey's.

Holliday, his lips set to their customary sardonic part, viewed the careless swing of her hips as she walked away from him and followed silently.

3

An hour or two later when they returned to the saloon, Kate saw that Holliday knew many of the men who frequented Shansseys. All greeted him with careful respect and none appeared to be a close friend. That was to her liking; she was all the friend he would need from then on, and since the bargain had to work both ways, he would be the only man sharing her bed henceforth.

Leaning against the long bar Shanssey had built along one side of the big room, she watched Doc as he sat in on one of the poker games already underway. There were four other players at the table and he was taking their money with an indifferent ease.

Elsewhere in the saloon the faro, monte and black-jack dealers were hard at it while the dance floor was crowded with sweating, stomping men and women all enjoying the fiddle and piano music despite the crowded conditions.

Shanssey had taken to Holliday immediately when they met, possibly because he was proud to have so famous a gambler making his saloon headquarters for his activities, or perhaps because it was prudent not to turn him away. There was a marked change in the tone of the games, for certain; the players, rowdies as well as the more refined gentlemen who sat in, were now restrained. Everyone adhered to the accepted rules and appeared to take the game seriously.

At the crowded bar, Kate felt an arm go around her waist and draw her roughly close. She jerked away, wheeled angrily. It was one of The Flat's better known residents, Ed Bailey.

"Drink's on me," he said, grinning broadly. "After that things'll be on you."

She pushed him away. "The drinking part's fine. The rest you can forget."

Bailey stared at her. "What the hell's that mean?" he shouted, raising his voice to be heard above the din. "You getting uppity with me?"

Kate smiled primly. "No, just happens I'm Doc Holliday's woman now. You feel like arguing about it, go do it with him."

Bailey swore deeply. "The hell with Holliday! My money's been good before."

"It ain't now—not yours, not anybody's," Kate said and moved off into the shifting crowd.

Other old and favored customers approached her as the night wore on. She turned them all away with the simple but startlingly effective statement, "I'm Doc Holliday's woman. You want to cross him?"

It worked like a shaman's charm and soon it was having not only protective but salutary results as well. Drinks came her way with no strings attached; she danced several times with men who heretofore had

18

felt they were at liberty to handle her as they willed, but who now addressed themselves to her as if she were an elderly, maiden aunt.

Kate quickly began to relish the pedestal upon which she was discovering herself, and for the first time in years she remembered what it was like to be respected and honored as if she were a woman of purity and status.

She smiled over the rim of her glass at Tom Truett, a trail driver boss who had called her to where he sat in lonely isolation at one of the tables. He was well into his second quart of whiskey and his tongue was a bit thick.

"That Holliday—he's a lucky bastard," he said. "If it was anyone else, I'd fight him for you."

The words were slightly muddled but the meaning came through to Kate and the thought occurred to her that it would be wise to do a bit of staking out on her part to prevent any claim-jumping in the days and nights to come.

Getting away from the drover after promising to return, she began making the rounds of the other women in the place. Drawing each aside she told them of her liaison with Holliday and made it clear that he was strictly off limits, being her personal and private property.

"I'll kill you quick as I'd mash a bug if you ever forget it," she declared, exhibiting the outline of the derringer in her pocket. "He's the first man I've ever taken a real liking to and I'm not about to let anybody queer it."

Erna, Christine, Candy, Maggie, Doll, and One-Eared Essie, all took the warning understandingly. Lottie Deno, however, was a different matter. She

19

pursued the profession with little gusto, preferring instead to gamble head-on with the men, something at which she was inordinately successful. Always a dark, mysterious sort of woman, she favored Kate with an enigmatic smile.

"He know about this?" she asked throwing her glance towards Holliday a few tables away.

Kate nodded, her eyes shifting to the gambler, too. He was slouched in his chair, pale features shining clean and sharp in the lamplight. An unlighted cigar was clenched between his teeth and the fingers of the hand holding his cards looked like tapering, ivory slivers.

"Ask him," she said coolly.

Lottie continued to smile. "Maybe I will. Aim to have him set in on the next game I get together."

Kate's lips tightened. Her understanding with Doc hadn't actually reached the state of mutual exclusiveness yet, as far as he was concerned. At the moment it was all on her part but the hour or two she'd spent with him in her quarters convinced her that, with a little more spade work, she'd soon have him in the same frame of mind.

"You ask him," she suggested quietly. "He tells you no, then you can use that knife you're carrying on me in any way you like. But if he says yes then I'll put a bullet in your goddamned head. That a deal?"

Lottie considered the offer for a long minute, and then shrugged. "Oh, the hell with it," she said, and moved off toward the faro table.

The crowd was growing steadily. Smoke and liquor fumes now were a blanket hanging beneath the rafters of the saloon, which seemed to fairly rock with the noise. A fight broke out on the dance floor and Mace, the burly, one-time Boston policeman whom Shanssey had hired to keep order, stepped in and roughly escorted the two combatants to the street.

Off and on as the evening progressed, Kate danced and drank with those who asked, but faithfully drew the line on anything further, making it clear she was now unavailable for such—try Candy or Erna or go on down to Nosey Kate's.

The strategy worked well and without a hitch until shortly after midnight when the big, barnlike building became filled to capacity. Smoke hung so low as to barely clear the heads of the restive patrons. The piano player banged away at the keys with full strength. He was the sole provider of music for the dancers, since the fiddler had long since slid under a table. All the games were still going full swing. It was then that John Shanssey sought out Kate and drew her aside.

"Customer's are doing some griping—some of them, that is. Claim you're pushing them off."

"I am," Kate said flatly.

The saloonman stared. "Since when? Was only this afternoon you—"

"Doc hadn't showed up yet."

Shanssey frowned and nodded slowly. "Then what some's telling me's for true—that you're saying you're Holliday's woman."

"Just what I am. Aim to keep on hustling drinks for you, but it ends there."

"Doc know about it?"

"Hell, yes, he knows about it!" Kate said, lying boldly.

Shanssey scrubbed at the stubble on his chin.

"Seems mighty fast. You didn't even know him 'till this afternoon."

"Maybe not," she replied sweetly, "but I'm one hell of a woman when I take the notion to be."

The saloonman was unimpressed. "Not sure I like this, Kate. You hanging around, and with him being what he is . . ."

"Be no trouble, and I aim to keep right on working the bar and the dancing."

"That all right with him?"

"Sure. Nothing wrong with doing that is there?"

"No, only there's bound to be some yahoo getting out of line."

"No sweat. I'll take care of myself. It won't get to him."

"Unless he decides to take a hand himself."

"He won't," Kate assured the saloonman. "You go on about your business. Don't fret over it."

Shanssey was quiet for a time, his gaze drifting out over the packed and milling crowd beneath his roof while he listened to the steady rumble of sound. Then, as if satisfied with what Kate had told him, he turned and moved off toward the blackjack table.

The game in which Doc had sat was breaking up, Kate noticed, and he was glancing casually about, inviting new players with his eyes while he absently shuffled a deck of cards between his long fingers.

She drew up suddenly. Shanssey had altered his steps and was heading for Holliday. He could have but one thought in mind. Moving hurriedly, she crossed behind the saloon owner and took up a position behind several men who were watching a nearby game in progress. She could hear but not be seen by either Shanssey or Doc.

22

"Doc—" Shanssey's voice had the quality of an apology.

Holliday turned lazily and looked up at the man. "You after your cut? Figured to settle with you when it came time to quit in the morning."

"Not that at all," Shanssey replied hurriedly. "Just want to ask you about Big Nose Kate."

Holliday's brow wrinkled slightly. He appeared to be tired but it was a resigned sort of weariness, and to be expected.

"Well?"

"Wanted to ask you about her."

"You know her better than I do. She got another name?"

"Calls herself Elder most of the time. Other times it's Fisher. Can't seem to make up her mind."

"I see. What about her?"

"Seems she's telling everybody you've moved in with her—that she's your woman."

Holliday took a drink from his bottle, as he considered Shanssey's words. "True," he drawled. "Least-wise the first part of it. Maybe the second. Not dead sure about that yet."

"You sure enough to lay claim, cut out everybody else that comes looking to bed her?"

Holliday drew a handkerchief from his inner pocket, coughed into it. Replacing the square of white cloth in his coat, he reached down for the pistol on his hip and fondled it thoughtfully. He carried another weapon, a razor-sharp, thin-bladed knife suspended in a sheath about his neck by a rawhide cord. The handle made a slight bulge in his shirt.

"Never yet met the woman I'd kill a man for," he said finally. "Could be someday."

"You've met her now!" Kate declared, pushing through the circle of listening men and facing him. "You're looking at her!"

Hands on hips, head thrown back, eyes snapping, the cloth of her dress pulled tight over the contours of her body, she challenged him defiantly.

He studied her, a mixture of admiration and amusement crossing his lean face. After a moment he smiled, slid the nickle-plated .45 back into its holster.

"Yea, I guess maybe I have," he said, rising. "And I expect it's something that ought to be celebrated. Come on, Kate Elder, we'll make a tour of the saloons in this burg, and do it up right."

4

"I've always wondered what it would be like to be a real lady."

Kate, sitting at a table with Holliday in one of the restaurants in The Flat a week or so later, spoke almost shyly.

Doc, barely touching the meal of eggs, bacon and biscuits before him, took the ever-present bottle of whiskey from his coat pocket, and dumping the water out of its tumbler, filled the glass half-full of liquor.

"Nothing wrong with you the way you are," he drawled.

She smiled at the compliment. That was one of the nice things about him, she thought. He was always the polite gentleman with her. To the outside world he might be a cold, dangerous man but to her he showed a side that was utterly different.

"Maybe, but I want more. I want to live in a fine house, go to church, take part in sociables, things like that. I'd like to be friends with rich, elegant people, be seen with them."

"Afraid you'd find it mighty boring," he said, staring off into the street. "It was a hell of a life."

Kate considered him for a long minute. Then, "That's what you came from, ain't it, Doc?"

He nodded morosely. "Came from—that's the right way to put it. I wouldn't ever want to go back."

"Your folks, were they the real uppity kind?"

"One of the so-called 'good families.' Landowners, plantation people. My father was a major in the army, and a lawyer. Fine man. Same goes for my mother. Fine woman."

"Why didn't you become a lawyer like him, instead of a dentist?"

"Expect they figured one in the family was enough. Besides, becoming a dentist was easier—that's what appealed to me. And fact is, I sort of like the work. Pretty good at it, I've been told."

"You think you might some day start being a dentist again?"

Holliday paused to cough, and swore at the inconvenience. He shrugged. "Hard to say. Still have all of my instruments."

Kate looked dreamily off through the dust-streaked window. "Mrs. Doctor Holliday," she murmured softly.

He shifted his partly closed eyes to her, a faint smile tugging at his lips. "Not the way you'd put it. Would be Mrs. John H. Holliday."

She repeated his words in the same absent tone. "Sounds so elegant!" she exclaimed, turning to him. "Doc, will it ever be that way?"

Holliday toyed with the nearly empty tumbler of whiskey, his lean fingers twirling it slowly. He was consuming a good three quarts during his waking

26

hours each day but the liquor seemed to have little effect on him.

"Doubt if you'd be happy living that kind of a life."

"I'm happy now being your woman, and nobody ever figured I'd tie down to one man."

He smiled. "How long's it been? A week? Ten days?"

"Don't see that it matters. I'm satisfied. Are you?"

"I am."

"It can go on this way forever, far as I'm concerned."

He smiled again. "Forever—that's one hell of a long time."

"Well, I mean it!"

The subject moved on to other things, the possibility of him taking over the gambling concession at Shanssey's, the advisability of moving into one of the new houses being built at the edge of town, the necessity of her again wearing a belt and holstered pistol instead of relying on the smaller, two-shot derringer—a matter on which they were in agreement. Other topics were discussed and then, the meal over, they returned to the saloon and by mid-afternoon the usual routine had resumed.

The days passed happily for Kate and fall turned to early winter. Holliday, always a cool, competent expert at whichever game he engaged in, be it straight poker, three-card monte, faro or blackjack, was a consistent winner. Their cash capital, which for convenience he and Kate shared equally and carried in money belts around their waists, increased steadily.

Shanssey was well pleased with the way matters had worked out and while there were still those old patrons of Kate's who resented her refusal to accommodate

27

them in any way other than dancing and drinking, no serious trouble ever developed.

As mates, Kate and Doc Holliday seemed ideally suited; although capable of soaring anger, he was ordinarily calm, imperturbable and exceptionally courteous. She was quick-tempered, hastily repentant and totally devoted where he was concerned. These opposites, mutually attracting, and combining with the false fires of fever burning within him and her quenchless passion created an alliance that no one, man or woman, had the audacity to challenge.

Late in the year Kate was sitting at a table in the saloon with two of the Calico Girls (so called because, like her, their services were limited only to being dancing partners and hustling drinks), when a stranger to all three appeared in the doorway.

Doc was having a conversation with the faro dealer at his station and Shanssey was behind the bar assisting the bartender in his preparations for the coming night. There were only a half a dozen patrons on hand, all more or less killing time until activity picked up.

The newcomer, a lean, stone-faced man with sharp blue eyes, flowing mustache and a direct, no-nonsense air to him, crossed to where Kate and the two women sat and halted before them. He was well dressed in a trim gray suit, polished cow-country boots and wide-brimmed hat.

"I'm looking for John Shanssey," he said.

Kate jerked a thumb toward the bar. "That's him. The one not wearing an apron."

The man bucked his head in a curt thanks, moved up to the counter. As her companions, Allura and

Trixie, fell to giggling and whispering excitedly about the handsome stranger, she turned to listen.

"John Shanssey?"

The saloonman paused. "Yeh?"

"Remember me? I'm Wyatt Earp. Like to talk to—"

"Earp!" Shanssey shouted, extending his hand, as he came around the end of the bar. "Good to see you again. Set down and have a drink," he added, motioning to the chairs at a nearby table.

They settled themselves and Shanssey beckoned to the barman for glasses and a bottle. "Been a long time."

"A long time," Earp agreed. "You still doing some fighting?"

"Nope. Gave that up after Cheyenne. That jasper cured me—hit me so hard my hair rattled. Anyway, found out I can make more money in the saloon business and it ain't so wearing on a man. What brings you here? Last I heard you were working in Wichita. Town marshal, I think it was."

"Deputy. Quit a time back. Working for the Santa Fe now."

"Railroad detective, eh?"

Earp nodded. "About covers it."

Shanssey refilled the glasses and waited for the lawman to make known his reason for being there. When Earp remained silent, he said, "You looking for somebody around here?"

"Dave Rudabaugh. Understood he was holed up in this area."

"Was," the saloonman said. "Pulled out quite a while back."

"Know where he was going?"

Shanssey shook his head. "Nope, sure don't."

29

Earp shrugged. "Sort of expected he'd be gone. Ought to be somebody around that can give me a line on him, however. Any idea who might help?"

Kate, only half listening, came to attention as Shanssey's reply.

"Doc Holliday—he'd be your best bet."

"Holliday—that damned killer—he here?"

The bar owner frowned and nodded. "He is, and if anybody can turn you a hand, it'll be him. Knows all the hard cases."

Wyatt Earp tossed off the last of his drink, turned the shot glass bottom up on the table. "Never deal with an outlaw. He's in the same class as Rudabaugh and his kind. I'd trust him no farther than I would them."

Anger lifted within Kate. Sharp words formed on her lips, checked as Shanssey made his stiff reply.

"Could be you've got him all wrong. Doc's a gentleman, and he's honest."

"He's also killed a half a dozen men—a half a dozen that we know of. Probably some we don't."

"Was a fair fight each time, the way I heard it."

"No doubt, but when a man's as fast with a gun as he is, the other fellow doesn't have a chance."

John Shanssey shrugged. "Can't blame him for being good. Been in no trouble since he showed up here."

"It'll come. Anyway, he's not likely to help a lawman."

Doc would be a fool if he did, Kate thought. Earp, plainly, was no friend and was not interested in becoming one. He regarded Doc as the worst kind of outlaw and unworthy of any consideration.

"You don't know the man like I do," the saloon-

30

keeper said. "I think he'll help you if I ask him to. Owes me a couple of favors."

Earp stroked his mustache and his hard eyes filled with skepticism. "Not sure I want to line up with somebody like him. Wonder, too, if I could rely on what he'd tell me."

"You could, but it's up to you. He's probably the only man around who can get the straight dope on Rudabaugh for you."

The lawman was silent for a long breath, then: "All right, see what you can do."

Shanssey rose at once. "Wait here," he said, and started across the saloon to where Holliday was sitting.

5

She didn't like Earp, Kate decided. He was too arrogant, too damned sure of himself, and he gave the impression that nobody was quite as good as he. Well, he was only a lawman, and Doc was a real professional, a doctor, so when you got right down to the grits, who was really the best man?

Shanssey's mention of Wichita had stirred her memory and she was recalling now what she'd heard about Earp. He'd cleaned up the town, had run out a lot of folks he'd tabbed as undesirables and clamped a lid on the livelier places, all without using his gun. She supposed he was a pretty fair lawman as lawmen went, but she doubted if Doc would care much for him either.

She glanced up. Shanssey, with Doc in tow, was coming toward her. He looked down as he strode by and gave her his slow, twisted smile. She shook her head warningly at him and he nodded and continued on to where Earp was sitting.

"Doc Holliday—Wyatt Earp," she heard the saloon-man say, making the introduction.

"My pleasure," Holliday said.

"The same," Earp answered coolly, and then to John Shanssey, "You tell him?"

"Only that I'd be obliged if he'd help you."

The lawman muttered something as Holliday settled onto a chair. Shanssey motioned to the bartender for another glass and while it was coming Holliday and Earp eyed each other appraisingly, saying nothing. The shot glass came. Shanssey poured drinks all around and lifted his.

"Here's to you both," he said.

Holliday nodded, tossed off his whiskey. Earp merely sipped at the glass he held.

"Looking for Dave Rudabaugh," he said when the toast was done. "John figured you might know where he went when he left here, or could find out for me."

Slouched in his chair, face tipped down, Holliday was studying the lawman through his heavy brows. "It's possible," he murmured.

"Want him for murder and robbery. I've chased him halfway across the country, cold trail all the way."

"Still a cold trail," Doc said. "Been gone from here for some time."

"Expected that, but I've got a hunch some of his friends are still around and know where he went. Be a big help if you'd get the information for me."

Earp paused and then when Holliday made no comment, added, "He a friend of yours?"

Doc's shoulders stirred. "No more than the next man coming through that door," he said indifferently, and turning aside, coughed quietly.

When the spell had passed he brushed at his lips

with a handkerchief and helped himself to another shot of whiskey. Earp considered him in icy silence. He was clearly irked at being forced to deal with a man he knew was an outlaw and therefore beneath his standing.

"Doc has connections," Shanssey said, breaking the tight hush. "Knows just about everybody that would have something to do with Rudabaugh. If anybody can find out where he's holed up, it'll be him."

But he won't, Kate assured herself. Rudabaugh doesn't mean anything to him but he won't bother to help a snotty bastard like Earp, especially since he is a lawman.

"You figure you can?"

Holliday nodded to to Earp. "Can try."

Kate came half out of her chair, an oath slipping from her lips. Allura and Trixie, who were still whispering and giggling, looked at her in surprise. She ignored them, and turning about, endeavored to catch Holliday's attention but failed, as his back was partly toward her.

He didn't owe John Shanssey that much, not by a damn sight! The saloonman hadn't favored him to such extent that he should help somebody like this Earp—a lousy badge-toter who'd turn on him in a minute if there was profit in it.

"I'll appreciate it," Earp said, his tone warming slightly. "Don't expect much, just some idea of where he most likely's hiding. Know that's what he's doing because he's aware that I'm on his trail."

Holliday poured himself another drink and refilled the small amount missing from Earp and Shanssey's glasses. Patrons were beginning to fill up the saloon as the mid-afternoon hour approached. Shanssey stood,

35

excused himself and moved off, leaving the two men to themselves.

At once Kate got to her feet and circled the table to Holliday's side. Earp viewed her from his cold eyes, nodding only slightly when Doc introduced her. He said nothing when she sat down in the chair vacated by the saloonman.

"Was there in 'seventy-three," he said, picking up whatever conversation that had been interrupted by Shanssey's departure. "Never much liked the place. Heard you did pretty well in Jacksboro."

Holliday said, "Was a good town for me."

He seemed to be enjoying Earp's presence and was really going out of his way to talk with him. They were a good deal alike, Kate noted, not only in the evident care each took in dress but in the way they spoke. Wyatt Earp had been pretty well educated, as had Doc, which probably was the reason he was taking to the lawman; Earp was one of his kind, a man on the same level.

She felt a stab of resentment at the realization. Schooling did make a difference, no matter what anybody said, and the higher the attainment, the more exclusive folks became. As for herself she'd gone no farther than a couple of years of high school. That placed her above most people she knew, but still well below Doc, who'd gone to college as well as the dental school in Baltimore that he mentioned now and then.

Earp no doubt had gone pretty far, too, and recognizing a fellow scholar, he seemed to be softening a bit and coming down off that lofty perch of his. That he was becoming more friendly somehow irked her.

"There's Ed and Casey Phillips," she said, looking

toward the door. "Expect they're wanting to set in a game."

The interruption had been deliberate. She was suddenly anxious to break up the meeting of the two men, instinctively seeing in Earp a threat to her relationship with Holliday.

Doc glanced over his shoulder at the two men and smiled wanly. "Expect they are," he said, pushing back his chair. "Care to play a few hands, Wyatt?"

The lawman shook his head. "Probably not be smart. Wouldn't want to get you into trouble with your friends."

"I can handle it," Holliday said easily. "Consider yourself welcome at my table any time. Rule of mine— I choose my friends to suit myself, not somebody else."

Turning away, he crossed to where Bailey and Phillips were drawing back their chairs. A third player was moving up to take a hand and fill out a foursome. On impulse Kate rose and hurried after Holliday. Catching him by an arm, she halted him.

"Doc, you're a fool if you help that Earp," she said in a hoarse whisper.

He studied her intent features thoughtfully. "Maybe."

"I—I don't trust him. He thinks you're dirt, and he'll cross you up first chance he gets."

"Seems a gentleman to me."

"That's all show!" Kate insisted, anger rising at the stubborn position he was assuming. "I heard them talking, him and Shanssey. He says you're nothing but an outlaw—a killer."

"Common knowledge. Never have denied it."

"Goddammit, Doc!" she exploded, losing her temper. "Not what I mean and you know it! He'll sell you out first chance he gets."

Holliday looked back. Earp had risen and was moving toward the open doorway. From nearby Ed Bailey called out impatiently.

"Come on, come on! Let's play poker."

"Suppose you leave Earp to me," Doc said quietly as he pulled away from her, and moved on to where the men awaited him.

Seething, smarting with the knowledge that Doc was ignoring her good advice, Kate wheeled and dropped back to the bar. Shanssey raised his glance to her.

"Something eating you?"

"That goddamned four-flusher you rung in on Doc—"

"Wyatt Earp?" the saloonman said, brows lifting in wonder at her agitation. "What about him?"

"He'll get Doc killed, or he'll do it himself, that's what! I don't trust him no farther'n I could throw a bull elephant."

"Earp's straight. He'd never cross a friend."

"Friend!" Kate snapped. "What makes you think he's Doc's friend? I heard what he said about him."

"Was before they'd met. Was different after Wyatt got acquainted with him. Seemed to like each other pretty good once that was over. But don't go growing any gray hair over Holliday. He can take care of himself."

"Could be you that gets him shot, too," Kate said, shaking a finger vigorously in the saloonman's face. "You think Rudabaugh and his friends'll let it pass when they find out Doc told Earp what he wants to know?"

38

"No point in hollering," Shanssey said mildly. "I'm thinking Rudabaugh or nobody else is going to pick a fight with Doc Holliday, no matter what. They'd be plumb loco to try it."

Kate impatiently brushed a stray lock of dark hair from her eyes and helped herself to a drink from a nearby bottle on the bar. Down the counter a few steps two men were watching and listening with interest. She flung them an angry look which turned them back to their own affairs. Again she faced the saloonkeeper.

"Just the same, Doc'll be a damned fool if he starts hanging around with Earp—and I'm blaming you for it if he does. Can only mean trouble and grief and it could buy him a bullet in the dark."

Shanssey paused and put his attention on Holliday, again caught up in a spasm of coughing at the table where he was playing. After a time he returned his attention to Kate.

"That temper of yours could get you in mighty big trouble, Kate," he warned in a low voice. "You try it on him and you'll maybe wake up real surprised."

"Doc'll listen to me," she said confidently.

"I ain't so sure he listens to anybody 'cepting himself. Take my advice, let things just ride along."

Kate gulped another drink, slammed the empty glass down onto the counter. "The hell with that! Earp's got you both hoodwinked, but not me. In the morning I aim to make Doc see that!"

6

The situation came to a head much earlier. Business fell off drastically around two o'clock, a phenomenon the frequency of which was beginning to worry John Shanssey. Tucking a full bottle of whiskey under his arm, Holliday made his way to the shack that he and Kate shared.

She was there before him, still in her garish saloon-girl dress, sitting primly on one of the chairs. He grinned at her, and after removing his coat and vest and loosening his collar and tie, he shed his boots and stretched out on the bed. She was angry, he knew; they had lived together for better than a month now, and possessing the quick, analytical mind of a born gambler, he had come to know her well.

"Drink?" he asked, uncorking the bottle and offering it to her.

Kate shook her head and watched him down a long swallow and lie back wearily, lips set to their customary sardonic smile.

"You're unhappy, I take it."

41

She drew up stiffly, eyes sparking. "Doc, you're a damned fool!"

"I suppose," he replied indifferently. "Just living's sort of foolish. Have you got some special reason for reminding me of it?"

"Wyatt Earp—that's what! He's using you, and he'll get you killed or maybe end up doing it himself."

"Nobody uses me," Holliday said, his voice taking on a slight edge. "As for killing, it's been tried a few times before."

"But you're trusting him and that's not like you! I heard you say a dozen times that you'd trust no man, never! Yet you trust him and he's a goddamned lawman. It'd make more sense if you said you trusted Dave Rudabaugh!"

Kate's color had risen with the tone of her voice and in the yellow flare of the single lamp setting on the table, her face took on a strong, bold look. Holliday regarded her silently through shuttered eyes, the corners of his jaws beginning to show whitely.

"You're wrong," he said finally, taking another sip from the bottle. "I've got Earp sized up as a square shooter."

"By God, I haven't!" Kate shouted, leaping to her feet. "And if you wasn't so pig-headed you'd know better! Why, everybody's thinking you're a sucker for letting him use you—a genuine eighteen-carat sucker!"

Holliday set the bottle on the floor beside the bed. Anger was now showing on his lean, pallid features and the brilliance in his eyes had heightened. Abruptly he seemed poised, coiled like a steel spring on the verge of being released.

"Drop it," he said in a voice cold as winter's wind.

"Drop it, hell!" she raged. "If you think I'm going

42

to stand by and let that four-flusher make a fool of you, you're crazy!"

"The shoe fits you better, lady, and I don't think you're so much afraid for me as you are jealous of him and our friendship!"

Kate swore, wheeled, snatched up an empty wash pan from the stand behind her and hurled it at him. Holliday jerked to one side. The tin bowl crashed into the wall and clattered to the floor.

"You figure you're so damned smart that you're never wrong!" Kate shrilled. "You don't think you can ever make a mistake!" Grabbing a fold of clothing awaiting the washwoman's attention, she threw it straight at his head. "You sure'n hell are making one this time!"

Holliday caught the clothing in mid-air, slammed it back at her and slid to his feet. Kate, the assemblage of shirts, petticoats, drawers and the like draped over her, cursed wildly and struggled to clear herself of the entanglement.

Her arms came free. She saw Holliday coming toward her, face grim. Clenching a fist she swung at his head. The blow caught him on the ear, staggered him momentarily. He caught himself and surged forward, now thoroughly aroused.

Catching Kate by the wrist, he swung her roughly about and sent her stumbling onto the bed, and then, both hands raised, he started after her. Kate screamed as she rolled to the edge of the bed. She saw the bottle of whiskey on the floor nearby, snatched it up and threw it. Holliday dodged, barely avoiding the missile, which shattered against the door beyond him.

Abruptly he halted as a wave of harsh coughing, induced by the furious activity, gripped him. He

43

stepped back, braced himself with one hand on the washstand, the other shielding his mouth. The seizure wracked him for a full minute and then for another period of time he simply stood there, weak and gasping, head down, while he waited for the return of strength.

Finally he straightened up and, crossing to the rack, took up his coat and boots and drew them on. Reaching for his hat, he turned to the door, paused and looked back at Kate. She met his gaze defiantly. There was no apparent diminishing of anger.

"Best you get this straight here and now," he said in a raspy voice. "Nobody picks my friends for me."

"That goes for me, too!" she yelled and, grabbing one of the pillows, flung it at the door as it closed behind him.

Kate listened to the thud of his boot heels as he walked down the hard-packed path to the saloon. When she could no longer hear it, she arose and began collecting the clothing scattered about the room. The anger within her was beginning to cool, but not the conviction that Wyatt Earp could mean nothing but trouble, perhaps even death for Doc. But she had failed to make him see it. She'd gone about it wrong, she guessed, but deviousness was no part of her make-up. Her thoughts and words were as direct as the fists she swung so effectively when the occasion demanded.

She should have handled Doc differently, she was realizing that now. He wasn't like other men she'd known, either those in passing or those who had tarried with her for varying periods of time. Ruthless killer and outlaw or not, he was a gentleman and would never respond to the tactics she ordinarily employed in getting her way.

But, dammit, he should listen to her! She had a little common sense even if she didn't have as much schooling as he'd had. He didn't own all the brains in the world. He should give her credit for some—and he ought to realize that she was only thinking of him. What the hell, if some bastard killed him, she'd have no trouble lining up with another man; fact was, once he was out of the picture and no longer around to be feared, they'd flock to her so fast and thick she'd have to beat them off with a club!

Kate paused, staring at the shattered glass on the floor and the wide, wet spot made by the whiskey. Getting the corn broom, she swept up the jagged pieces, opened the door and tossed them into the weeds growing in the yard, taking a moment as she did to listen. Music was hanging faintly in the cold night air. It was coming from one of the other saloons, one farther down Griffin Street.

On impulse she propped the broom against the side of the hut and bent her steps toward Shanssey's, a slight worry tugging at her mind. Entering the strangely quiet building she glanced around. Ernie, the bartender, was lounging against the counter talking with Tom Willis, one of the Indian agents. Lottie was at one of the tables playing cut-throat with two cowhands, and over in a back corner Allura was dawdling over a bottle with a drummer in a derby hat. Doc was nowhere to be seen.

Well, it'd be a cold day in hell before she'd go chasing after him! She'd never thought that much of any man and she wasn't about to change. Wheeling, Kate returned to the cabin, undressed and crawled

45

into bed. He'd come in when he got tired and sleepy enough—and when he did he'd find nothing but a cold shoulder waiting for him.

She awoke around mid-morning and lay quietly staring at the wall for a time. Then, suddenly remembering, she rolled over. Doc was not there beside her. He hadn't come back. She got up and dressed slowly while a fresh flow of anger began to build within her. Damn him! Who the hell did he think he was, treating her like that! Like as not he'd spent the rest of the night with one of the girls at Nosey Kate's. Well, by God, two could play that game! It worked both ways!

Dressed, gun strapped about her waist, she simmered furiously as she hurried to Shanssey's. Within her was a faint hope that she'd find him there curled up in one of the chairs but such hope died immediately when she entered. The saloon was empty except for two men who were lazily going about their cleaning duties. She gave it all a bit of thought and then stepped up to one of them.

"You seen Doc Holliday?"

The man stared at her blankly and wagged his head. Kate wheeled and flounced through the doorway into the street and crossed to the restaurant where they ordinarily took their meals. He was not there. Suddenly feeling alone, she sat down at their table and ordered a pot of coffee. She'd wait. He just might come.

An hour later he appeared in the entrance, haggard and drawn, the usual slow smile on his lips. Wordless, he walked to the table and sat down opposite her. There was no apology in him and he gave no indication that he expected one from her. He simply and

46

totally ignored last night's incident as if it had never occurred.

"Thought you'd like to know," he said in his quiet way, "I found out that Rudabaugh's at Fort Davis. Told Earp about it. He's gone. Left here an hour or more ago."

Relief ran through Kate. Wyatt Earp was out of their life now; she could forget about him and the strong attraction he held for Doc. Their quarreling had been for nothing.

"Good riddance," she said tersely, and then in a more gentle tone, "You look all in. I think we'd best get back to the house so's you can rest."

"I'll live," he countered, taking the inevitable bottle of whiskey from his coat pocket and setting it on the table before them. "Right now I can use a plate of eggs and bacon to go with my drinking."

7

Except for one thing, life in The Flat resumed its normal routine for Big Nose Kate and Doc Holliday. The covenant had been broken and now she no longer felt obligated to reserve her considerable charms only for him and in the days that led into December she slipped easily back into the old custom of taking to bed any virile and attractive man that caught her fancy.

Holliday didn't seem to care much, and if she was hoping to stir the flames of jealousy within him, the tactic was a miserable failure. He took note, shrugged and concentrated on the cards while spending more and more time in Shanssey's than was customary.

"I've got no claim on you," he said one cold evening as they sat at a table in the rear of the nearly deserted saloon. "Correspondingly, you have none on me. We're just two people living together, enjoying each other's company—or did."

"Whose fault is that?" Kate flared instantly, and

before he could reply, contritely added, "Guess it was as much mine as yours."

He shrugged. "We're both human, and misunderstandings happen. All to be expected."

"It would be different if we were really married," she said quietly.

Holliday did not look up, but slumped in his chair, chin sunk in his chest. He reached for the bottle on the table before him and poured himself a drink. Studying the amber liquid briefly, he tossed it off.

"That's not for me," he said. "I'd be a fool to marry. I have to take my living day by day, and I'm never sure whether tomorrow'll come or not. I won't put you or any woman through that."

Kate looked at him closely, a softness slipping into her eyes. An expression of tenderness was a rarity with him: only occasionally it would seep through the cold veneer which he exhibited to the world.

"Maybe she wouldn't mind, Doc—"

"She'd be a fool not to. Life's tough enough without taking on something like that."

"Not always the way it is. Can be some good things to remember. We've had a few."

His mouth pulled into a hard smile. "It's the good things folks always remember and the bad they forget. I suppose that's how it should be. God knows there's little enough happiness around."

She started to reply and hesitated while he weathered a fit of coughing. After he had brushed at his lips with a handkerchief and soothed his throat with a drink, she spoke.

"I'll say it again—I wish we'd get married."

The conversation had turned him inward, funneled

50

him into one of his dark and sullen moods. He swore impatiently.

"Forget it. You don't know when you're well off."

"Holliday!"

At the imperious call, Doc turned his attention to the center of the saloon. Ed Bailey was settling down at one of the tables while motioning two other men to join him.

"I'm cleaning you out tonight, Holliday! Come on, let's get at it!"

Doc shrugged, smiled faintly at Kate. Bailey was a loud-mouth and a drunk, a man she knew he cared little for, but his money was as good as anybody's. She watched Holliday rise, cross the floor to where the three men waited and take his place. Cracking a new deck, he waited for the ante, shuffled the cards and placed them in front of Bailey.

"Cut," he said coldly.

"This time you're up against a real card player, not one of them greenhorns you've been fleecing," Bailey said in a loud voice as he divided the stack. "You can make up your mind to that."

Holliday smiled inscrutably and dealt the cards.

Kate, aware of a sudden tenseness in the room, got to her feet and moved over to the bar. There were no more than a dozen persons in the place and all at once they drifted in close to the players, where they could better observe the game. Frowning, she turned to the bartender.

"There something going on, Ernie?"

He bobbed his head. "That Bailey, he's been shooting off his mouth about Doc. Says he's going to break him, show him up for a tinhorn. Brought along some of his friends to watch him do it."

51

Kate's shoulders lifted and fell. "He'll learn. End up busted flat like all the others that got the same idea."

"Ed's primed for trouble, though. Just like him to try winning by using his gun."

A frown tugged at Kate's forehead. She had never doubted doc's ability to take care of himself. Time and again she'd heard men say that he was the fastest man with a pistol they'd ever seen—and the most deadly. There'd been a few who had disputed the opinion, none of whom lived long enough to admit their error to bystanders. Still, Ed Bailey was a sneak, a cheap trickster, and he had a lot of admirers who just might take it on themselves to lend him a hand.

Pulling away from the bar, she moved to where the game was in progress. Already the pile of currency and coins in front of Doc was large. He had evidently benefited handsomely from Bailey as well as the other players in just a few hands. At the moment he was again shuffling the cards, his eyes on Ed Bailey, brighter than usual and filled with amusement.

"The game going on?" he asked.

"You're goddamn right it's going on!" Bailey shouted.

"You'll be needing more cash," Holliday said, indicating the depleted pile in front of the man. "I don't take chits."

"I'll get it! Plenty of folks around here'll stake me if I ask. Deal the cards."

Holliday proceeded. The man next to him opened, threw away two cards and drew the replacements. Bailey called for three, the second player two. Doc stood pat. The bet went the circle and stalled at Bailey, who studied his hand while he idly fingered the discard pile.

Holliday frowned. "Play poker," he said in a low voice.

Bailey swore, threw down his hand. The man with the openers showed his pair of kings. Doc took the pot with three tens.

The deal passed, went around again, and once more Holliday was forced to warn Bailey about thumbing in the discard. The man to Doc's left added his protest.

"You play your way, I'll play mine!" Ed snarled, angrily throwing down his hand. He was losing steadily.

Elsewhere in the saloon everything had come to a standstill. Incoming customers had bypassed the bar and added their presence to the three-deep ring surrounding the players. Kate had improved her vantage point by climbing onto a chair. Others were getting the idea.

Bailey played out the last of his cash and rashly helped himself to the small pile of the friend to his left. It was his deal and he opened immediately, tossing out a gold half eagle.

Holliday and the man next to him stayed and drew their cards. Bailey filled his hand, again taking time to consider while he riffled the discard. Finally he raised the opening bet, Doc watching him coldly all the while. He met the raise and the two remaining players dropped out. Bailey, grinning broadly, laid down his cards. Three queens.

"Beat that!" he yelled exultantly.

"I have," Holliday replied, and tossing his hand into the discard without showing it, raked in the pot.

"The hell!" Bailey shouted and reached for his gun.

Holliday's arm swept up. Lamplight glinted dully off the blade of the knife he carried about his neck. Bailey, weapon only half raised, fell back, blood gushing down his shirt front.

For a long breath there was nothing but silence in the saloon, and then a strangled voice broke the stunned hush.

"Get the marshal—somebody! Doc's cut Bailey wide open!"

8

Kate dropped from the chair on which she stood and elbowed her way through the suddenly hostile crowd to Doc Holliday's side. His features were dark and expressionless, reflecting no particular feeling one way or another.

"Ed didn't have a chance," someone muttered.

Kate saw Holliday raise his eyes and stare coldly into the direction from which the comment had come. She laid a hand on his arm. He seemed not to notice. He rose slowly to his full height while his right hand swept back the skirt of his knee-length coat to reveal the nickel-plated .45 hanging at his hip. "If any of you want trouble, I can supply it," the gesture seemed to say.

"Was Bailey's fault," Ernie the bartender said. "He tried to throw down on Holliday, was too slow. Doc got him with a knife."

Kate turned. The bartender was speaking to John Shanssey. The saloon owner nodded.

"Bound to happen. Ed's been spoiling for trouble

55

ever since Holliday hit town. You send for the law?"

"Yeah," Ernie replied and glanced toward the doorway where several men were hurrying into the room. "Coming now."

Doc, deliberately, methodically, was collecting his winnings at the table. The coins made chinking noises as he stacked them and dropped them together with the paper money into the soft leather poke he used for that purpose. Directly across from him the body of Bailey slumped in a chair, shirt front covered with blood.

"Who is it?" the lawman asked crisply, pushing his way through the growing crowd.

"Ed Bailey. That gambler—Holliday—knifed him," someone volunteered.

"Was pure self-defense, Marshal," another man added. "We all seen it."

"Seems it always is where he's concerned," the lawman said drily, halting beside Bailey. Giving him a perfunctory glance, he swung his attention to Doc who was now standing with arms folded across his chest as he waited in cool silence.

"What started it?"

"He kept fooling with the deadwood," Ernie explained, pointing at the discard. "Holliday warned him to keep his hands off but he didn't pay no mind. Then when Holliday took the pot without showing his hand, Ed made a grab for his gun."

The marshal nodded slowly and looked about at the crowd.

"That how you all seen it?"

The player from whom Bailey had borrowed money shrugged. "Was no need to kill him," he said. "Ed was a little drunk and maybe getting loud but he'd never a used his gun."

"What makes you think that?" the lawman demanded. "Mistake he made was going for it. Far as I can see, Holliday was in his rights. He ain't no mind-reader."

"Something we ought to let the vigilantes decide!" a voice in the back of the room shouted.

A chorus of approval went up. The marshal moved to Holliday's side, his young face serious. "Don't like the sound of this. Bailey's got a lot of friends and they just might get something started. Might be better for me to lock you up till morning. You agreeable?"

Doc listened to the mutterings of the crowd for a few moments. His lips twitched in resignation. "Was self-defense. Happened just the way you've been told, but if you figure it best——"

"I do," the lawman said decisively. Drawing his weapon, he bucked his head at his deputy. "We'll put him in that room in the hotel, let this simmer down a mite. Clear the way."

Kate stepped up close to Holliday. He frowned as the marshal lifted his weapon from its holster, and then, shrugging, fell in between the two lawmen as they carved a path through the pack of onlookers. When they reached the doorway he looked back at her.

"This'll be all right. See you in the morning."

She gave him no reply, but a deep worry was mounting within her as she stepped aside, out of the way of the noisy crowd trailing the lawmen and their prisoner. John Shanssey's voice reached her.

"That bunch——they're the ones that've been hanging around Bailey. They won't be satisfied until they stir up a lynching party."

"Doc will be safe there in the hotel," Kate said, but it was more a question than a statement of fact.

The saloonman brushed at his mustache. "Maybe, but I'd feel better if he was locked up in the jail at the county seat. Hotel's no more'n a cracker box."

Kate, abruptly taut, lips tightly compressed, whirled, stepped through the doorway into the cold night and fell in behind the crowd, now gathering in front of the hostelry. The marshal was standing on the steps, both hands raised, palms forward as he endeavored to quiet the shouting and make himself heard. The deputy was apparently inside the flimsy building guarding the door of the room in which Doc had been put.

"He ain't nothing but a murderer!" a man's voice shouted. "We ain't letting him get by with killing Ed!"

"Don't belong around here anyhow!" another yelled. "It's them outsiders that always causes trouble."

"Right! Time we was letting them know they're not welcome!"

"Best you get out of the way, Marshal. Let us take care of him!"

"No!" The lawman's shout was a desperate sound barely audible above the hubbub. "The man deserves a hearing, if you don't agree it was self-defense."

"What difference that make? Ed didn't have a chance against him."

Kate, worry now gripping her tightly, turned away. She was shivering from the biting cold but it went unnoticed. It had been a mistake for Doc to let the

58

marshal arrest him, lock him up. It was clear now he was not safe in the custody of the law, for, as John Shanssey had said, the hotel-room jail was little better than nothing at all, and if the lynch fever caught hold there'd be no stopping the mob.

Which was how it would be. Bailey's friends would keep at it until they had the crowd sufficiently worked up to storm the hotel, take Doc from the room where he was being held—and if they didn't, the Organized Vigilantes, who were on a town improvement crusade, would. Either way Doc would be the loser; he had no close friends, being the sort of man who cultivated none, actually wanted none, and thus had only her to stand for him. And what could she do to stop them?

Thoughtful, she reached the saloon, stepped up onto the landing and paused just outside the entrance. Shanssey, Ernie, several of the women and two or three customers were nearby, watching the activity in front of the hotel. The gathering there had increased now to where it entirely blocked the street, and the yelling and shouting were so loud that what was being said was drowned in its own din.

"He'll never see daylight," Ernie said heavily. "That bunch of crazy bastards are like wolves. They're smelling blood and nothing's going to stop them."

Kate came to a sudden decision. Moving on, she passed them by unnoticed and entered the saloon. Bailey's body had been carried off to the undertaker's and now one of the cleaners was scrubbing away the blood that stained the floor.

Continuing on out to the rear of the building, she hurried to the cabin and began to collect their more important belongings and pack them in their two bags. After placing the cases on the bed along with a pair of the woolen blankets they had been using, she drew on her heavy coat and returned to the street.

9

There was no time to lose. One glance at the gathering in front of the hotel warned her of that fact. Running, keeping in the shadows so as to not attract attention, she hastened to the livery stable a short distance off Griffin Street.

The night hostler there was Earl Peavey, and with a silent prayer on her lips that he was still on duty and not down among the crowd, she entered the structure and stepped into the office. She had lent him money once when he was in trouble and he'd sworn to never forget the favor. Now, with no one else she could turn to, she was calling on him.

"Kate! What're you coming here for?"

A sigh of relief ran through her: he was there. She hurried up to him. "Earl, I need your help."

There was a small, pot-bellied stove in the center of the room and the heat it threw off was making the small quarters stifling.

"Help from me? Why, sure."

"I need two horses all saddled and ready to go."

Peavey scratched at his ragged whiskers. "You needing horses—what for?"

"Don't ask me any questions. Just do what I say if you want to be my friend."

"Yes, ma'am, you can bet on that. It's whatever you say."

"I want you to bring them to me. I'll be waiting down at the creek—that place where there used to be a log bridge."

The hostler nodded and again clawed at his whiskers. "This got something to do with all that hoorawing going on down the street?"

Kate nodded but made no explanation. "I need a gun, too. Will you sell me yours?"

Earl turned, took a belt and holster filled with a cedar-handled. .45 from a peg and held it out for her to see.

"Got this'n. Ain't mine. Belongs to a fellow that left it here for us to sell."

"It shoot all right?"

"Sure does. Tried it myself."

"I'll take it," Kate said and hung the belted weapon over her shoulder. "One thing more—you know that shack where I live?"

"One back of Shanssey's?"

"That's it. There'll be a couple of bags and some blankets on the bed. When you start down to the creek with the horses, pick up that stuff, bring it along."

"Sure. When you wanting all this done?"

"Soon as you can. Not long until daylight and it's got to be by then."

"I'll be there waiting for you. Ah—uh—about the paying. The horses and gear, they belong to Mr.

62

Granger. And that gun, like I said, it ain't mine else it'd cost you nothing. I got to account for—"

"You have how much it is all figured out, Earl, and when I meet you in the morning, you'll get paid. Be a little extra for your trouble."

"Now, Kate, you know that ain't needful."

"You'll be doing me a big favor and I want to show you I appreciate it," Kate said, backing toward the door. "Something else. Don't say a word about this to anybody, and most of all, don't fail me."

"Don't you worry none about that. I'll be there just like you want," the hostler promised. "And there ain't a soul going to know about it."

Back in the street Kate halted. Preparations were made for a hurried getaway—now came the part part, that of freeing Doc from his improvised jail cell in the hotel. Whatever, it would have to be done soon. There were two groups now, she saw, swinging her attention down Griffin. The crowd, for some reason, had split. Likely one bunch were the friends and followers of Ed Bailey, all yelling for immediate vengeance. The others could be the more tractable citizens who were paying heed to the marshal—or they could be the Vigilantes.

Immediately she wheeled and dropped back to the alley that ran behind the row of buildings to her left until she came to the rear of the hotel. Still without a plan, she tried the door, cursed softly when she found it locked. Doubling back to the corner of the building, she made her way along its side until she reached the street.

The milling assembly was about out of hand. The marshal, alternately threatening, begging, promising, was having no luck in pacifying Bailey's sympathizers, and the demands for vengeance were getting stronger. Give or take a few minutes, within the hour it would be all over for Doc Holliday.

Anxiously Kate chewed at her lips. If only she could get inside the hotel without being seen! She'd have a chance then to seek out the room where Doc was being held, disarm the deputy guarding the door, and free him. But it was impossible; it required passing in front of the crowd, as well as close by the marshal, and entering the building in full view of all. Recognition would be instantaneous.

And in the state of mind the blood-hungry mob had worked itself into, that could be the spark that set off an assault on the hotel. She needed some means for diverting their attention.

Fire! That was it! The Flat, like all such hastily constructed boom towns, was nothing short of a tinder-box. If she could get a good blaze going somewhere the mob would forget Doc for a few minutes and turn their attention to fighting the flames. That every resident did his part at such times was a generally accepted requirement, for fire was an enemy of all.

Cutting back to the alley, Kate followed along its littered, irregular course until she spotted an old, weathered shed off to one side. It should burn fast—and bright. Turning into it, she pulled up in surprise at seeing a horse tied to the remains of a manger at one end. Jerking loose the neck rope, she led the animal outside, sent him off in the direction of the hotel with a slap on the rump and returned to the sagging old structure. Again inside she scraped together a fair-sized pile of straw and trash and banked it against one wall.

A match . . . Panic hit her briefly as she dug into the pocket of her dress for one of the sulphur sticks she ordinarily carried to light the cigars of customers. It was empty. Trembling from both anxiety and cold, she probed the other pocket, but relaxed as her fingers came in contact with two of the slim slivers. Glancing about to be certain no one was near, she scratched one of the matches into flame, and hoarding it carefully, applied it to the tinder. It sprang to life immediately.

She whirled quickly, darted through the doorway and raced down the alley to the opposite side of the hotel. Staying close to the shadow-struck wall, she worked her way to the front. Before she reached the building's corner a yell of alarm went up.

"Fire! Fire!"

Smiling tightly, Kate paused at the edge of the landing. The crowd, galvanized into action by the shout, shifted, broke, and began to flow toward the flaming shack. Without hesitation, Kate swiftly crossed to the doorway and ducked inside, missing by only a step the clerk and two customers who were hurrying to do their part in facing the emergency.

The deputy marshal had drawn a chair up in front of the door behind which Doc was imprisoned. He came to his feet at her approach.

"Big fire out there!" she cried. "They're needing your help."

The young lawman shook his head. "Marshal told me I was to stay put no matter what."

Kate smiled sweetly. "You got new orders," she said, leveling one of the pistols at him. "Open up or I'll blow a hole in you."

The deputy wasted a breath or two staring at her,

and then reaching into his shirt pocket, produced a key, inserted it into the lock and released it.

"Inside—without the shotgun," she ordered, and backed the lawman into the room.

Holliday, sprawled comfortably on the bed, came to his feet, grinning broadly. She handed him the belt and gun she'd acquired from the hostler and motioned toward the doorway.

"Got to get out of here—fast!"

Holliday snatched up his hat and coat and followed her into the hall. Pulling the door shut, he locked it, and threw the key off into the darkness of an adjacent room.

"Now what?" he asked as she led the way to the rear of the building.

"Got everything set for us to get away, but first we've got to make it down to the creek without somebody spotting us."

He nodded and silently trailed along behind her as she unlocked the hotel's back door and stepped out into the alley. A hundred yards farther on the flames of the shed were beginning to lower as a bucket brigade industriously sloshed water over them.

The fire was under control and would soon be out. Already the more persistent members of the mob were drifting back to the street. It would be only minutes until the deputy managed to attract someone's attention and word of Holliday's escape would be known.

Hurrying through the smoke-filled darkness, they reached the creek and took up the path that ran along its winding course to the old bridge. Kate was hoping Peavey would be early. Things had cut a bit finer than she'd anticipated and abruptly they had run out of time.

66

She halted. There was no sign of the hostler. Holliday drew his coat tighter about himself and looked at her inquiringly.

"Why are we stopping here?"

"Friend of mine's bringing horses and our duds. We're a little early but I thought maybe he'd be here anyway."

A wry smile pulled at Doc's mouth. He glanced off into the direction of the hotel. Shouts were rising into the pale gray of approaching dawn.

"Better be pretty quick or we'll sure be in the soup —both of us this time."

"Miz Kate?"

Earl had evidently been nearby all the while, but had simply waited to be certain. She heaved a sigh.

"Over here," she answered.

The hostler came forward at once, moving quietly through the willows. He was leading two horses. The bags and blankets hung from their saddles.

Kate crossed quickly to the nearest mount, unhooked her bag from the saddlehorn and, placing it on the ground, released the catches.

"Told Earl we'd settle up for the horses and that gun I gave you when we got here," she said to Holliday as she drew a pair of trousers and a shirt from her case. "Like for him to have a little extra for his trouble, too."

She heard Peavey protesting quietly and then caught the sound of chinking coins as Doc counted out the necessary money from his leather pouch. When he had finished squaring up she had changed clothing and was now dressed as a man, even to a pair of heavy shoes.

67

"Thank you, folks," Earl said, moving off. "And good luck wherever you're going."

"Thanks to you," Kate called after him.

She stepped over to her horse and waited while Doc helped her to mount and affix the suitcase where it would ride smoothly at the rear of the saddle. Then, after securing his worn carpetbag to the horn, he swung onto his horse. Passing one of the blankets to her and draping the other about his shoulders, Holliday nodded to her. In the cold, gray winter light her face was a pale oval.

"Owe you plenty," he said. "My life, in fact. Makes where we go now your choice."

"Dodge City," she replied promptly.

Four hundred miles in the distance—on the other side of the Indian Territory; a trail where they could expect to encounter not only hostile redmen but the worst of outlaws. Doc Holliday only smiled.

"Dodge City it is," he said.

10

Sunrise found them a good distance from The Flat and bearing steadily north. There was no way of knowing if a posse was on their trail but they took no chances and pressed their horses hard for the first two hours.

The day was cold with a clear, blue sky bending overhead and there was little wind. Since there had been no opportunity to lay in a stock of trail supplies, they did not pause for meals. In fact, they gave the matter little thought until late in the afternoon, when they drew to a halt on the banks of the Brazos for night camp.

They had seen no one during the course of the journey, no other pilgrims, no ranchers, and of course at that time of the year, no cattle drives. Nor had they caught sight of any riders coming after them from the south. So they assumed they had gotten away from The Flat clean and need have no worries about the Vigilantes or Ed Bailey's vengeful friends.

"You make 'til tomorrow without grub?" Holliday

69

asked as they hunched over a small, warming fire. "If not we'll keep going. Bound to come across somebody along the river."

There had been little conversation between them during the day, both being intent on putting as much ground between themselves and Griffin Street in as short a time as possible.

Kate shrugged. "I can stand it, can you?"

Holliday took a bottle of whiskey from his pocket, smiled. "Long as I've got plenty of this, I'll make out." After pulling the cork, he passed the liquor to her, and watched as she had a swallow. Then he took his own drink.

"Going to be cold sleeping out here," she said then, drawing the blanket tighter about her body.

He grinned again. "Can stand that, too, long as I've got you with me," he said and tossed another handful of dry wood into the flames.

It was a bitter, seemingly endless night they spent locked together in the two blankets, mutually warmed by each other's bodies. They were awake well before daylight, and after breaking the chill that gripped their bones with a good fire, they mounted and rode on, still headed northward.

Shortly before noon they reached a small settlement. There was no restaurant, and heading for the one saloon along its short street, they treated themselves to a complete meal. When it was over Doc laid in a fresh supply of whiskey and then both visited the general store where they outfited themselves with warmer clothing, as well as a larder of food, selecting things that would require little or no cooking.

Neither cared for kitchen duty, especially on the trail, and they were agreed on the decision to get by

70

with a minimum of such and do their eating, whenever possible, in the towns and camps along the way.

The little buckskin mare that Kate was riding and Holliday's chestnut came in for their share of attention, too. During the stop they were stabled long enough to enjoy a ration of grain and a thorough rubdown by a hostler.

They stayed that night by the Red River with the Indian Territory awaiting them on the stream's opposite bank. Again, except for their brief stop-over in the settlement at midday, they encountered no one. It was simply too cold to be traveling.

With morning a cold wind blew in, and because of the scarcity of wood, they had a poor fire and began the day sitting in their saddles, trembling with cold despite the woolen blankets wrapped about them.

At noon they were forced to halt in the shelter of a butte and escape for a time the biting edge of the ceaseless blowing. They were able to build a fire and eat a little from their supply of food, washing it down with whiskey, which helped considerably.

"You want to stay here for the night?" Holliday asked. "Cold but at least we'll be out of the wind."

Kate smiled, shook her head. Doc was again as she'd first known him, attentive, thoughtful, always looking out for her comfort and best interests.

"I'd as soon go on. Maybe we'll come to a town where we can spend the night."

"Not out there," he replied, gesturing toward the reddish, rolling flats extending in all directions. "We're in the Indian Territory."

She was quiet for a time, listening to the gusting sound of the wind in its passage. Then, "How much farther to Dodge?"

"Good four days, I expect. Never rode into it from this side."

"But you've been there."

"I have. Fact is, I know quite a few people in the place." He paused, took a swallow of whiskey and continued. "You serious about wanting to start a new life, being like the society people and such?"

"It would be wonderful, Doc. Why?"

"Just thinking—Dodge might be just the town to make a new start in."

Kate stared into the fire. She was realizing now that to make such a change would be a big step. When she had voiced the wish before it had seemed simple. You just stopped living one way and began living another.

"Do you think we—I could do it?"

Holliday shrugged. "Why not? Expect we're what we make ourselves."

She nodded slowly. "I'd like to try, Doc, and I would, real hard."

He made no reply, took another pull at his bottle and then drew the blanket more closely about his lean frame.

He had endured few severe coughing spells so far on the trip and that puzzled him. Was it due to the tenseness of the past hours or did it reflect the wisdom of the Atlanta doctor who had told him of the advantages of dry, fresh air? He guessed the medical man had been right. Away from the smoke and fumes of the saloons, the long hours indoors, he was breathing easier. He doubted, however, that it would make any difference in the long run.

"Best we move on," he said rising. "Don't know

exactly where we are, but we can't go wrong if we keep heading north."

Helping Kate onto the saddle, he tucked the blanket about her and mounted his horse, taking time to cover himself as much as possible with his own woolen cover. They rode out, bearing straight into the teeth of the relentless wind, cruelly scouring the flats and the rolling hills with a knife-sharp edge.

Camp that evening was made in a small grove of trees rearing like a gray thumb in the center of a vast, empty world. Mercifully the blow died at sunset and they were spared that disagreeable affliction. Both were bone tired, and after a quick meal of crackers, dried meat and canned peaches, fortified as usual with whiskey, they turned in, again wrapping themselves together, cocoon-like, in the blankets.

Kate did not immediately fall asleep despite her weariness. She was still thinking of Doc's words, of what he had said about starting a new life in Dodge City. He had not declared the intention in so many words, but had only walked around the edges of the possibility as if trying to make sure it was what she wanted.

It was. She'd had time to think about it and knew now that, given the chance, she could become a lady and live respectably and take her place among proper society. When Doc broached the subject again she'd not hesitate; she would tell him that it was what she wanted—if he brought up the matter again, she amended as she dropped off to sleep.

Near midnight Holliday, coughing deep and raggedly, awakened her. Separating herself from him, she hurried to get one of the canteens and forced him to swallow a little water. He was alternating between chills and fever, trembling with cold and seemed, to her, unusually weak. It frightened her but there was little she could do other than feed him water and whiskey, which to him seemed to be a cure-all for every malady.

After the spell had passed and he had quieted, she again drew the blankets about them and held him close for the remainder of the night. Her own warmth appeared to relieve the chill that convulsed him, and toward the morning, he slept.

When she awoke again she found him up, apparently none the worse for the severe attack, warming bread and meat over the fire. While she was still in the blankets he brought breakfast, such as it was, to her, and paused to watch her eat.

"Obliged for last night," he said with his twisted smile. "Doubt if I'd ever made it without you."

She could think of no reply, continued to chew on the tasteless meat and scorched bread. Then, "I was scared."

His shoulders stirred indifferently. "No need to be," he said turning back to the fire. "When it comes, it comes and nothing will make any difference."

He seldom mentioned the disease gnawing away at his lungs. It seemed he preferred just to ignore its existence.

"Isn't there anything you can do about it?"

"No, and a long time ago I stopped thinking about it. As somebody once said, nobody's going to get out of this life alive."

"But there should be something—medicine maybe?"

He shook his head, reached for his bottle, patted it gently. "This is the only medicine, far as I'm concerned. The doctor did say a dry climate might help."

"Then we ought to go there wherever it is."

Holliday swept the broad country with his glance. "Can't find one much dryer than this."

Not long after that they rode on. The day warmed to some extent, and thankfully, the wind did not blow again. They made good time and when darkness overtook them they were watering at the South Canadian.

Camp that night was the most comfortable they had experienced since leaving The Flat, and reveling in the glow of a roaring fire once their simple meal was over, they both relaxed. They were not too far from Dodge City now, and all in all, they had fared well, with weather no worse than the icy wind, the cold no more intense than was to be expected and they had encountered neither outlaws nor Indians.

"I figure you're my good luck, Kate," Doc told her expansively, lighting up a cigar. "Things've gone right for me ever since we teamed up."

"You're forgetting Ed Bailey."

"The bad luck went to him. My good luck was you being around, getting me out of there before they could put a rope around my neck. Owe you for that, and for last night, and I don't forget favors."

"You don't have to—" Kate began, and broke off suddenly.

Her eyes were reaching beyond him while color drained slowly from her features. Holliday, sprawled on his folded blanket, read the fear on her face. He let his hand stray to the pistol at his side, as he leisurely turned his head. Three Indians stood at the edge of the firelight, their coppery skins reflecting the glow of the flames.

Without looking back to Kate he said, "Reckon I

was counting the pot a little soon," and then to the night visitors added, "What do you want?"

"Cold—"

At the sound of the guttural reply Holliday sat up, drawing his weapon covertly and keeping it out of sight beneath his leg. He nodded.

"Come close and get warm."

The braves moved in eagerly and crowded about the fire. All were young and dressed in cast-off army uniforms. Each was carrying a discarded military rifle. After a few minutes the one who had spoken bared his teeth into a fixed grin.

"Whiskey—you give?"

Liquor and Indians didn't mix. Holliday had heard it said often and knew it to be a fact, but the bottle was there on the blanket before him for all to see, and with the odds all wrong and the possibility that there could be more braves off in the darkness, he was not of a mind to press matters. Besides, there wasn't much liquor left, probably a drink for each of them. Picking up the bottle he handed it to the nearest of the three.

"No more," he said.

The Indian seized it greedily, tipped it to his lips and downed a swallow. Instantly the buck next to him wrenched it away and held it to his mouth. The third man waited long enough for him to gulp his portion, then claimed the balance. The bottle empty he threw it off into the darkness and turned to Holliday.

"More?"

Doc slid the pistol into view and began to toy with it. "No more," he said. "You go."

The Indians glared at him for a long breath, abruptly wheeled and faded off into the night. Instantly

76

Holliday rolled out of the fire's glare and came to his feet, listening intently. Shortly the quick tattoo of running horses came to him. Heaving a sigh he returned to where Kate, her own pistol out now and ready, sat on her blanket.

"Gone. Lucky they were only beggars. Could've meant plenty of trouble," he said, crossing to his saddle and taking a full bottle of whiskey from one of the bags.

Kate continued to stare off into the direction in which the braves had ridden. "Aren't they liable to come back?"

"Doubt it," he answered, settling down again. "If they do we'll handle them somehow."

Opening the bottle he offered it to her, and when she refused he took a long, satisfying drink himself and once more stretched out.

"Breaks are still going my way. We run into Indians, they turn out to be friendly. Kate, you're right for me, like I've said. I'm going to make it up to you."

She smiled quizzically. "What's that mean?"

"You say you want to be like other people, lead a regular life? All right, that's what it'll be. We get to Dodge, we show up as Dr. and Mrs. John Holliday. I'll open my dental office again, quit gambling and you can go about the business of being a fine lady. How's that sound to you?"

A warm glow suffused Kate, one not provided by the campfire. "It's sounds wonderful, Doc. Wonderful."

11

Late in the afternoon two days later, they rode into Dodge City, taking the time after crossing the Arkansas to halt briefly and make themselves presentable. By dark, a boarding house having been located and suitable rooms rented, they registered as Dr. and Mrs. John H. Holliday, and settled in.

He would have waited until morning to do more toward the attainment of the respectability that Kate sought, but she pointed out the lack of anything in her decimated wardrobe suitable for a woman of quality to be seen in, and so while he disposed of the horses, she visited the several ladies' shops and acquired what she felt was proper dress.

Later that evening in their quarters, Holliday watched as she tried on her different purchases and paraded them before him. She was a handsome woman and he told her so.

"Maybe if looks will do it, I'll have a chance," she said a bit wistfully.

"No reason why not. As Mrs. John Holliday, the

wife of a professional man, you should have no trouble getting acquainted with the town's best people."

"But how do I meet them? I just can't walk up to some elegant lady and say, 'Howdy, I'm Mrs. John Holliday, the wife of the dentist.' "

"I'll see to that," he assured her.

The next morning, after a leisurely breakfast in the boarding house, Doc took the short walk down to Front Street and its adjacent counterparts, both above and below the Deadline, and made a tour of the town. The Alhambra, Delmonico's Restaurant, The Dodge City Opera House, The Alamo Saloon, The Lady Gay and the Long Branch where he'd heard Luke Short was running the gambling concession, were just as he remembered them.

He encountered a few familiar faces, but he was more or less a stranger in Dodge insofar as personal appearance went, and he was hopeful that his name had not become so heralded that it would make difficult his plans to become a successful practicing dentist— something he had noticed Dodge City seemed to lack.

Scouting further, he located a small building that would serve admirably for an office and rented it on the spot. He proceeded then to outfit it with a few necessary pieces of furniture, hired a man to clean the premises and engaged a sign painter to letter the window. Later, after he'd arranged to have the equipment he'd stored at The Flat freighted in, and put to use, he'd drop by the *Dodge City Times* and take out an advertisement. Meanwhile, he'd get his practice underway without benefit of newspaper announcements and with what tools he'd brought along.

Satisfied with what he'd accomplished, Holliday retraced his steps to the Long Branch to slake his thirst. As he stood at the bar of the almost deserted saloon, he glanced about and turned to the bartender.

"Chalk Beeson and Bill Harris still own this place?"

The bartender nodded. "Yeh, still do. You a friend of theirs?"

"Know them. Name's Holliday."

The aproned man drew up in surprise. "Doc Holliday? You looking for a game?"

His reputation had preceded him. Holliday shrugged. It was as good a time as any to make known the change in his way of life.

"No, opening my office. I'm a dentist. Intend to follow that line from now on. Maybe I'll set in on a gentleman's game once in awhile."

"You mean you're quitting the cards?" the bartender asked incredulously.

"I'm a dentist," Holliday repeated, "and a damn good one. Be obliged if you'll pass the word along."

"Sure, sure," the man behind the counter murmured, shaking his head slowly as if unable to believe what he had heard.

Finishing his drink, Doc turned to the door, paused to cough discreetly into his handkerchief, and continued on, stopping at all of the other saloons to make his presence and purpose in Dodge City known. It was early and few of the regulars were about, but he left the message as he had at the Long Branch, knowing that it would receive full attention.

When the rounds were made he then headed for the office of the city marshal, that position being held, so he'd been told, by Bat Masterson's brother, Ed. The news of his arrival was there ahead of him. The lawman greeted him coldly.

"Things are fairly quiet around here, Holliday. I'd as soon you'd keep going."

"You'll get no trouble from me," Doc replied curtly. Evidently Masterson was unaware of his plans. "I'm opening my office—dentist."

The lawman frowned. "This straight talk?"

"A fact. Already rented a place."

Masterson gave that consideration and finally shrugged. "Long as you stick to dentistry I won't have any objections."

"Doubt if that would make much difference, anyway," Holliday said quietly. "Bat around?"

"Somewheres out in the county. He's the sheriff now. Likely be in this afternoon."

"Might mention what I've told you."

Masterson nodded, "I'll do it. You and him ever get things patched up?"

"Nothing to patch up far as I'm concerned," Doc said and took his leave.

He returned to the office and found the painter at work lettering his name on the window. The sign that would hang over the door stood propped against a wall drying. Satisfied that all was progressing as expected, he went back to the boarding house. Kate was anxiously awaiting him.

"Is everything all set—your office, I mean?"

Holliday smiled, sank into a chair and reached for the bottle on a nearby table. After taking a short drink, he said, "Everything. Even been over to the marshal's and got squared away with him."

"Then you really mean to do it?"

He stared at her. "Said so, didn't I?"

"Yes, but I was afraid that once you got here and saw your friends . . ."

"That I'd change my mind? Not a chance. You want respectability, you're going to get respectability. Tonight we're dolling up and taking in the Comique Theatre. Some New York actor putting on a show there. Heard he was real clever. Afterwards we're going to Delmonico's and have us a late supper. That's the style among the upper crust. Then tomorrow night we'll go to the Opera House. Between the three places you'll have rubbed elbows with the town's best people."

Kate sank onto the edge of the bed. Her eyes were starry. "I—I can't believe it's true, Doc," she murmured. "I just can't believe it."

"Well, it is," he drawled, lips set to their usual cynical twist. "I hope it's what you want."

Being a lady, or trying to be, was difficult, and there was a notable lack of excitement to it, Kate discovered. It was necessary to be dressed just so, to always be on guard while she was speaking, not to say anything that would shock the good women of the Missionary Society or the Dodge City Ladies Social Club. Liquor, of course, was out except in the confines of her and Doc's quarters, and then only if she was not scheduled to attend some function, the importance of which grew less and less as time wore on.

And there were those with whom she was never able to make friends even after a proper introduction. That she was the wife of Dodge City's only dentist cut no ice with them; she was an outsider and they made it very clear that an outsider she would remain.

Doc, too, had changed. Never much of a talker, he became more close-mouthed than ever; he brooded to the point of sullenness a great deal of the time. His de-

pressed mood came mostly from the steady deplet-
ing of his financial resources, she knew. The dental
profession was not a lucrative one, at least in Dodge,
and he undoubtedly thought often of how, with the
turn of a card in a poker game, he could make more
money than he would in months practicing dentistry.

By the first of the year gentility had begun to pall
and the siren call of the saloons with their pulsating
noise, gay laughter, moments of tension and friendly,
smoke-filled atmosphere, was becoming louder. But
Kate refused to listen and despite personal inner tur-
bulence steadfastly maintained her hard-won position
among those who had accepted her as Mrs. John
Holliday.

She was feeling particularly down that spring day,
and decided to do something about her doldrums.
Dressed in the dove-gray suit that Doc liked so well
and wearing a perky hat, she left the boarding house
and headed for his office. She needed company, some
one to bolster her beseiged and faltering determina-
tion, and persuading him to squire her to Delmonico's
for the noon meal seemed a good solution.

Reaching the office on one of the side streets, she
opened the door and entered. There were no patients, and the man she saw standing in the doorway that led into Doc's private quarters where he had
set up a sort of laboratory she took to be a drummer
peddling dental supplies. Anger flashed through her
when she recognized him. It was Wyatt Earp.

He said something to Doc, turned and moved by
her. Touching the brim of his hat, he said, "Missus
Holliday," in a faintly amused and derisive tone and
stepped out into the street.

Kate, abruptly seething for no other reasons than

84

her dislike of the lawman and the accumulation of frustrations that possessed her, marched stiffly into the back room. Doc was refilling one of the two glasses setting on a small table. Evidently the two men had been hashing over the days in The Flat and she had arrived just as the reunion was breaking up.

"When'd he get here?" she demanded.

Holliday's eyes narrowed. He raised his glass to his lips and completed his drink. "Yesterday. Masterson got to Rudabaugh ahead of him. He's trailing some other jasper now."

"He planning on staying in Dodge?"

Holliday refilled his glass. Kate, fuming, began to move about, pace agitatedly back and forth. Outside, from somewhere below the Deadline, a spatter of gunshots broke the hush. Immediately the thump of bootheels sounded as men hurried by enroute to investigate.

"Well, is he?" she pressed. "If he is maybe you ought to have him move in with us. Then you could spend all your time with him."

"Now, that's a right good idea," Holliday drawled. "But fact is he's just passing through. On his way out of town when he stopped by."

"And you're wanting to go with him! You're not fooling me, Doc. That's what you'd like to do. I know it and you know it. You're sick of this dentist thing."

He studied her thoughtfully. "And you're tired of playing at being a lady."

"Yes, by God, I am! I've got a belly full of being respectable. I want to go back, live like I used to."

"You'll stay out of saloons as long as you're around here," he snapped. "People know you as my wife, as

Mrs. John Holliday. I won't having you dragging my name through the dirt."

"Is that so?" Kate shot back airily. "Well, Mister Doc Holliday, I'll damn well do as I please! If I'm good enough for you by one name, I'm good enough for you with another!"

Holliday's eyes had taken on a fine brilliance, and the corners of his jaws stood out whitely. Tossing off his drink, he smiled sardonically.

"Respectability didn't last long."

"I'm fed up with respectability!" Kate shouted, jerking off her hat and hurling it against the wall. "So are you—own up to it! You're running out of cash and those two-bit card games you set in on with the town muckity-mucks don't bring in enough to pay for your whiskey! Why don't you come right out and say you're ready to quit, too?"

"Not denying it," Holliday replied. "Fact is it wasn't me that wanted it in the first place. It was you."

"Well, I'm done with it now. I'm going back to where I can have some fun and enjoy myself. If you don't like the idea, best thing you can do is trot right out after your friend Earp."

Holliday lunged to his feet, eyes snapping, lips working angrily. Slamming the empty glass he held to the floor, he shook a long finger at her.

"Had enough of this about Earp! He's got nothing to do with us—or me! That clear?"

Kate, back against the wall of the narrow room, nodded stubbornly. "All right, but I'm still going back to working in a saloon!"

"Go back. See if I give a goddamn! But you remember this, Kate; people around here think you're my wife, and as long as they do I won't have you peddling yourself to every man that offers you the price!"

She was calming under his fury. "Sure, Doc, whatever you say. Just want to start living like we used to, having fun, things like that."

It had not been Kate's intention to abandon her mantle of respectability when she entered Holliday's office, but seeing Wyatt Earp there and hearing his quiet, contemptuous salutation, had triggered the release of a steadily growing desire she had carefully ignored. Finally it had been brought out into the open.

But she was pleased now, glad that it was all over, glad that the decision to return to the sort of life for which she was meant had been made. Now it could be as it had been for them in The Flat, and the fact that Doc had agreed so readily was proof enough that he had been longing for the excitement of those days and nights, too.

12

Kate swung back into the old routine with gusto, dividing her time between Dog Kelley's Alhambra Saloon and the Long Branch, with an occasional stint at the Alamo. Generally, she chose to be where Doc was, and since Beeson and Harris, the owners of the Long Branch, and Luke Short, who oversaw the gambling in their establishment, were friendly toward him, he made it his principal field of operation.

He did not forsake his dental office entirely and that troubled her somewhat. She'd thought he had taken up his original profession merely to enhance her position in the sort of life she had thought she wanted. It was evident now that he actually enjoyed following it and perhaps would have continued had she not made such a positive stand. But he was again in the big money and she knew that did much to soothe the pangs of loss.

As the lethargy of winter was dissipated and spring approached, Dodge began to stir with the expectations of the coming cattle drive season and the booming business that always accompanied it. Doc got to where he spent less and less time in his office and more and more at the Long Branch.

It became just as it had been at The Flat; the two of them up all night, she enjoying herself as a dance hall girl on the floor, at the bar or sitting at a table shilling drinks, while Doc, lean features pale in the smoky lamplight, took on any and all comers at poker.

Then with the approach of dawn, it was home to their rooms at the boarding house where they slept until midafternoon or so. Rising, they loafed about, took their time dressing and then went finally for a meal at Delmonico's or one of the other restaurants. That done, the next item in order was a leisurely stroll about town.

Kate found these meanderings particularly enjoyable and took great pride in the deference that men encountered displayed toward Doc, a civility notably lacking among those to whom he was known as simply, Dr. J. H. Holliday, dentist. But here, among their own kind, he was Doc Holliday, gambler, gunman—deadly killer—and all possessed a healthy respect for him.

She stuck to their bargain insofar as being known as his wife was concerned. She never permitted her lusty zest to go beyond the bounds of mere comradeship with the patrons who frequented the saloon where she happened to be.

"I'm Doc Holliday's wife," she would say to the more amorous ones, and at once ardor would cool perceptibly. No one cared to cross the lean-faced, hard-eyed man who spoke little but cut so wide a swath in the bustling cowtown.

His reputation had long since caught up with him

and no man cared to be the next name added to the list of killings credited to him. In that aura of reflected glory Kate basked contentedly.

And then again came chance.

"Ed Masterson cashed in his chips," Doc informed her one afternoon as they were having the usual combined breakfast and dinner. "Some cattleman from east of here, I'm told."

A shooting was nothing unusual insofar as Kate was concerned, but Dodge had been fairly quiet and orderly since their arrival.

"Who's going to be the new marshal?" she asked merely in the interests of conversation.

"Charlie Bassett, most folks figure. Would be a good job for Earp if he was around."

Kate bristled slightly and shrugged. There had been no mention of the name since the blow-up in Doc's office and she had all but forgotten the man.

"What did they do to the jasper who shot Ed?"

"Haven't caught him yet, but Bat's out after him. Whoever he is, I doubt he'll get far. Bat's not the kind to give up, and Ed being his brother, he'll work extra hard at bringing him in. That drummer I saw cozying up to you last night, put a check rein on him."

Kate looked up in surprise. She hadn't realized Doc was even aware of the incident. Horace Green, his name was, and he was a ladies' ready-to-wear salesman for some concern back east. He had come on pretty strong, but he was pulling out for Wichita. He had even tried to persuade her to come with him. He dropped the idea when she told him who she was.

"Sure, but don't fret over me. I can take care of

myself," she said, pleased at discovering Doc possessed a jealous streak where she was concerned.

He muffled a spell of coughing in his handkerchief and drank a half a tumbler of whiskey to ease the stress. He said, "See that you do. Don't want to remind you again that around here you're my wife."

Kate smiled with pleasure. "You won't need to. I like being Mrs. Holliday and I aim to keep it that way. How'd you do at the cards last night?"

"Not good. Luck seems to be down—has been for a week or more."

It was disturbing him and so brought a frown to her brow. "Maybe we should move on. Heard things were going big up Colorado way. Lot of new mining towns."

"A thought," he said, refilling his glass. "Luck can go sour sometimes if you hang around one place for too long. I've had it happen before. If things don't change, we might just push on."

The days rocked on. Doc's fortunes continued to lag and he became morose and more uncommunicative than was usual. They quarreled frequently and eventually Kate's patience began to wear thin.

"Let's get the hell out of here!" she exploded one morning after a particularly bad squabble. "We don't have to stay. We can go on to Colorado, or back to Texas. It won't matter to me which. Point is, I don't like the way things are going with us."

"Not ready to give up yet," he replied perversely. "Gone through downhill slides like this before, and there always came a day when my luck changed. It will again."

"But you said we were about broke."

"We're not far from it, but I can always get a stake

from Luke or Dog Kelley, if I'll agree to work at the Alhambra."

"Maybe you ought to go back to being a dentist for a spell."

It had been weeks since he'd been to his office and as a result his practice had dropped to nil.

"A bit too late for that, and besides I've found out people don't like a man coughing over them when he's working on their teeth. No money in it, anyway. Half the patients I took care of never got around to paying their bills."

The door of the cafe opened and Town Marshal Bassett, frowning darkly, came to their table. He nodded to Kate, faced Holliday.

"Doc, hard for me to say this, but I've got a complaint against you."

Holliday leaned back in his chair and considered the lawman in wonderment. "Complaint? Over what, Charlie? Sure haven't won any big money lately so it can't be my gambling."

"Not that. A store up the street got robbed. Owner claims it was you that done it."

Holliday rocked forward, stared at Bassett. "I did what?"

"Says he seen you doing it."

Doc shook his head slowly. "Been down on my luck of late for sure but I haven't got to where I'm robbing storekeepers. You can tell that man, whoever he is, that he's a goddamn liar."

"What I figured, too. Was supposed to have happened night before last, around daylight."

"You can tell that bastard that he's a liar for me, too," Kate said, coming to Holliday's defense. "He was home in bed with me."

Bassett bobbed his head. "Well, we'll just let it ride. Expect the real hold-up man'll turn up. Doubt if that counter-jumper'll be of a mind to press charges, anyway."

"You know where to find me if he does," Holliday said, reaching for his glass.

The marshal turned and left the restaurant. Kate looked closely at Doc. "Wasn't you that robbed that store, was it? I remember you didn't come straight home the morning Charlie's talking about."

Holliday swore. "Hell yes, it was me!" he snarled. "Got myself a whole hatful of cash, blew it all on whiskey and women. That what you want me to say?"

"I don't give a goddamn what you say!" Kate shot back angrily.

Somehow the conversation had turned, become taut, for some reason she could not fathom. She had been only joshing him, but with things going the way they were for him, he was touchy. To believe that he'd bother to rob some two-bit merchant was ridiculous. He was simply in a dark mood and she should make allowances, show a bit of understanding.

"I'm sorry, Doc," she said, rising. "Let's forget it. I'd like to take a walk down along the grove."

He was on his feet, shaking his head, his ire gone as swiftly as it had come. "You go on. I'm dropping by the Alamo, try my hand there. Maybe it'll bring about a change."

"It's still early—"

"New bunch of marks in town—passing through. They don't pay any attention to time." He paused, gave her a slanted look. "You be at the Alhambra or you figuring to see your peddler at the Long Branch tonight?"

94

"At the Long Branch," she replied instantly, perverseness having its way with her.

The brilliance came into his eyes and his mouth pulled into a set line. "Let me remind you once more who people think you are," he said in a grinding voice. "The other half of our bed belongs to me. I'll stand for no other man crawling into it. Understand?"

Temper flared through Kate. She had already assured and reassured him of that fact. The question was now becoming somewhat shopworn.

"I'll do what I damn please!" she shouted.

Other patrons in the cafe looked around in surprise. The cook and his waitress came from behind the partition that blocked off the kitchen from the dining area and stared at them curiously.

"Not while you're calling yourself my wife," Holliday said in a lower voice.

Kate glared at him hotly, brushed her napkin angrily at her lips. "Oh, go to hell!" she said and turned for the door.

Knocking it open she stepped out onto the landing, but drew up short. Coming toward her was Wyatt Earp. "You again!" she snapped.

He smiled, touched the brim of his hat with a forefinger. "Was told I'd find you and Doc here. He still inside?"

Kate nodded curtly.

"Fine. Want to give him the news. I just signed on as deputy marshal here in Dodge."

"You what?"

"Took on the job as Charlie Bassett's deputy—"

Anger billowed up within Kate and overflowed. "Well, that's just fine!" she shouted. "You and Doc

95

can really get cozy now, and when you see him tell him I said he's all yours!"

Earp studied her quizzically, not understanding either her anger or her words.

"I'm pulling out, leaving it all to you two, in case you don't know what I'm talking about," Kate raged, and wheeling, walked hurriedly toward the boarding house.

If she was lucky Horace Green had not gone yet. She'd catch a ride with him to Wichita and let Doc sweat a bit.

13

The trip from Dodge City to Wichita with the clothing drummer had been uneventful, except that he had spent considerable time looking back over his shoulder somewhat apprehensively for the first few hours. The distance was a little more than a hundred and fifty miles but the time required to cover it, because of several stops Green made to interview customers, consumed a full five days and nights.

Having dutifully paid her fare en route, Kate bid Horace Green goodbye when he let her out of his buggy in front of a hotel on Douglas Street, and then, a smile tugging at her lips, she watched him scurry away, still fearful that the notorious gambler and killer, Holliday, was on his trail seeking vengeance on the man who'd made off with his woman.

For the first and second day she had entertained such hope herself, but by noon of the third she had abandoned it. Had Doc taken it in mind to follow and reclaim her, he would have put in an appearance by then.

She wasn't giving up on him yet, however. Let a full week slide by and the situation would change. Doc was a man with no real friends; actually he had no one close other than her. Being the solitary sort of man he was, it wouldn't take long for him to feel the pinch of loneliness and start needing her. Then he would come.

Perhaps . . . Wyatt Earp was back in Dodge, she realized, back to stay—a permanent resident. Kate's jaw tightened as she considered that. Where Earp was concerned, Doc was like a child in the presence of a father whom he greatly admired, almost worshiped. With the lawman around all the time Doc just might forget all about her.

She tried to shrug off thoughts of that possibility as she made her way to the Palace Saloon, where she'd heard an old acquaintance, Trixie, could be found. Rowdy Kate's place had long since been closed down by the law, she remembered, and with its demise there was no one else in the settlement that she could think of other than Trixie.

She noted as she entered that the Palace was an orderly, almost dull place at that hour of the day. Halting just within the batwings, she glanced about, her practiced eye taking in the dozen or so men playing cards at the rear of the room, the three or four others lounging at the bar. A moment later she spotted Trixie and hurried toward her.

Her friend, a large blonde with the shadow of a mustache showing on her upper lip, rose at once and, rushing forward, threw out her arms.

"Kate—as I live and breathe!"

"It's good to see you again, Trix," Kate said, responding.

The card players had paused, and the patrons at the bar as well as the aproned man behind it had all turned to look, sizing up the newcomer with interest. Kate was fully aware of her appearance; she had put on her dove-gray suit that morning to travel in and it set off her figure to its best advantage. She smiled, nodded to all.

"What're you doing here in Wichita?" Trixie asked as they sat down to the table.

"Looking for work and a place to stay."

The blonde woman frowned. "You? What happened at Dodge? Heard you'd married Doc Holliday and was living high on the hog."

"We never did get real married. Just told folks that. Guess we would've got around to it someday if things had gone right."

"That mean you and him've split up?"

Kate nodded. "He's a hard one to live with. Gets down in the mouth and the devil himself can't get along with him. Finally got my fill of quarreling with him and took off when his friend Earp blew back into town. Doc treats him like he was God Almighty Himself and forgets all—"

"Earp? Wyatt Earp?"

"Yeah, you know him?"

"Know him!" Trixie exploded. "He's the jaybird that closed everything down here in Wichita! Was a deputy for a spell and he sure made it hard on all of us."

"He's taken on the same job at Dodge."

Trixie shook her head sadly. "Well, it's good-bye Dodge City then. Inside a month he'll have it dead as it is here in Wichita."

Kate remained silent. She had her doubts that a

99

man could do to Dodge what had been done to Wichita—not while there were men like Dog Kelley and Chalk Beeson and his partner Bill Harris, plus a score or more of equally influential men running the town and benefiting from the way it now was. Wyatt Earp might just find out he wasn't as big a wheel as he thought!

"You think I could go to work here?" she asked, glancing about. The contrast of the Palace to the Alhambra or the Long Branch was immense. You could ordinarily find more people in those two places when closed than were presently in the Palace.

"Sure, why not. I'll square it with Bill York. It's his place. You can bunk in with me if you like. Got plenty of room."

"As soon be by myself if I could. Expect you understand."

Trixie shrugged. "Up to you."

"There any other girls?"

"Just me and Charlie. Charlotte her real name is. She's got herself a shack at the edge of town. Widow. Trying to raise a couple of kids." The blonde paused, and studied Kate thoughtfully. "Not going to be like it was in Dodge. Best you don't expect much."

"Can see things aren't very lively."

"All we get're a few cowboys and railroad hands and drummers and now and then some of the local bigwigs out to paint the town red. Palace is the best saloon in Wichita, if I do have to say so myself. Just set easy for a couple of minutes."

Trixie rose, crossed to the bar and, drawing the aproned man standing behind it aside, spoke to him. Kate saw him glance at her and nod, after which the blonde turned and retraced her steps to the table.

100

"It's fine with Bill, and he says you can have the room next to mine. He's got just one rule, don't roll the drunks."

"Never have," Kate said a bit stiffly. "Don't need to."

"Figured that but I wanted you to know. Come on, I'll show you where you'll be staying."

There were never more than two dozen patrons in the Palace at any one time during its busiest hours, except possibly for an occasional Saturday night when the count might go a bit higher. Being a new girl on the premises, Kate did not lack for attention and for a while she had no time to brood over the fact that Doc apparently cared so little that he had not bothered to come for her.

He would know where she'd gone, since she had taken pains to leave word at the boarding house where they lived for anyone who might make inquiry as to her whereabouts. "Anyone," of course, referred to Holliday; he would be the only possible man with real interest. If he did ask, she finally got around to admitting to herself, it had been out of curiosity, for as the days and nights passed and he neither appeared nor sent word asking her to return, it became evident that he had no intentions of doing so.

Life in Wichita began to pall. It was all too tame for her and a restlessness began to set in. She had expected Doc to reclaim her; he had not and that was a blow to her ego. She thought she meant more to him than that, for he had indicated as much many times, but that was before he had become acquainted with Earp.

Goddamn Wyatt Earp to hell anyway! It was all his

101

fault. He was the one who had changed Doc and turned him from her. She hoped somebody one day soon would put a bullet in his head and rid the country of him. Then maybe she and Doc could get together again.

As she strolled among the scattered tables of card players that night, a familiar face drew her attention. She considered the man for a time, unable to place him, and turned finally to Charlie, who was nearby.

"That john in the blue shirt—I know him but I can't remember his name."

"That's Jim Earp," Charlotte answered promptly. "Drives a hack. Comes in once in a while."

Kate looked more closely at the man. "He some kin to Wyatt Earp?"

"Brother."

"Goddamn him," Kate said bluntly and moved off leaving Charlie staring after her in wonderment.

That same night she had news of Doc. A whiskey drummer in from Dodge City, remembering her from The Flat, took a shine to her at once. After a few drinks and a whirl or two on the near-deserted dance floor, they retired to her room.

"You run into Doc Holliday when you were in Dodge?" she asked.

The peddler shook his head. "Heard he'd gone to Colorado—Leadville, I think it was. Big mining boom going on up there."

"Earp go with him?"

"The marshal? No, he's still in Dodge." The man hesitated, remembering. "Say, that's right! I'd most forgot. Was you and Doc Holliday that left The Flat

102

in a hurry last winter. Something about a killing he'd done."

Kate was only half listening. Doc was in Colorado and by himself, or at least without Wyatt Earp. Maybe she had misjudged the situation; maybe they weren't such close friends after all, or possibly they'd had a falling out.

Why then hadn't Doc come for her so they could go north together? That was hard to understand. She frowned and gave some thought to packing up, making the trip to Leadville. A new town, a new place, maybe they could start all over again. One thing, if they did, she'd be a bit more patient with him this time. She'd try to understand him better.

"Somebody said he didn't stay there long," the drummer continued. "Guess things wasn't as good as folks claimed. Usually the way it works out. Ain't never like rumors have it."

"You know where he went from there?" Kate asked in a falling voice.

"No, sure don't. Now, if you're real interested in finding him, drop a letter to Marshal Earp in Dodge City. If anybody knows it'll be him."

A surge of unreasonable anger flooded through Kate at the suggestion that she ask a favor of the man she so thoroughly hated.

"I'm not about to ask that bastard anything!" she cried, suddenly turning upon the startled man and shoving him from her bed. "Now you get the hell out of here and don't ever speak to me again!"

14

The summer was a hot one in Wichita, which only served to make the time more tedious for Big Nose Kate. The town saw only a few of the cattle drives that were in full swing, and she spent countless hours thinking of how it would be in Dodge, trail's end for most drovers.

There would be hundreds of cowboys roaming the streets below the Deadline and crowding the saloons. Music would be in the air and every dance floor would be crowded with whirling, stomping couples all having a gay old time.

Over in the areas reserved for gambling, men would be slouched in their chairs; layers of smoke would be hovering above them in the soft, yellow light of the chandeliers while, faces impassive, eyes narrowed, they studied the cards they held and made their decisions to call or bet.

Doc. How many times had she stood by him and watched fascinated at the absolute nerveless manner in which he worked. A thousand dollars on the turn of a card, and win or lose, it never showed on his pallid features. Once, in The Flat, she had seen him bet five thousand on a hand, lose, and then shrugging, assemble the deck and say quietly, "Gentlemen, I believe it's my deal."

He was a natural gambler: she had come to that conclusion soon after they'd met, and it was clear now that whether he loved the profession of dentistry or not, he could never give up the cards and the life that went with them, although it was the worst possible calling he could follow considering the disease that plagued him.

Night after night he'd sit in the sunless, smelly confines of a saloon, sleeping only briefly and then during the day when complete rest was impossible, eating irregular meals of dubious quality—and always with copious amounts of whiskey. He drank as much as a gallon in a day and no one ever saw him when there was not a bottle within easy reach of his slender fingers.

Strangely, if his health did not prosper, it grew no worse. The doctor in Atlanta had given him two years of life at most, he'd told her once after recovering from a particularly hard coughing spell. Thus he was on borrowed time and one day it would all catch up with him regardless of how he lived or what he did or did not do.

Accordingly, he reasoned, it was only good sense to fill his numbered days in whatever manner he deemed most suitable and satisfying. That was what made him so dangerous to other men, that bitter disregard for life, that complete disinterest in whether he lived or died. Certain death lay somewhere in a

106

future that could embrace one hour, one day, one year—or ten.

It wasn't that he courted the end as did some she knew who were expert with a gun. Indeed, he hoarded life with a stolid passion but he would not deny the inevitability of its end. When it came, it came, and if in his remarkable ability to stave it off he failed, so be it. All this she had understood, had catered to and never opposed. And it had worked well.

"Oh, Doc!" she moaned softly. "I was a fool to leave you. I—I want to go back."

"You talking about Doc Holliday?"

Kate, sitting alone in the center of the near empty saloon, looked around. It was late summer and while brooding over the past she had been cooling herself with one of the cardboard fans a local mortician had distributed about town. She hadn't intended her thoughts to become vocal, and now to cover up the vague embarrassment that filled her, she shrugged.

"Oh, I know him," she said flippantly.

"Going great guns in Dodge City," the man said, hitching his chair closer to her. "Just came from there a couple of days ago."

Kate restrained her eagerness. "That so? Didn't know he was back."

"He sure is. Took a hand in quite a little ruckus the marshal had there a week or so back. Saved his life, in fact."

"The marshal?"

"Wyatt Earp."

Her spirits sagged never lower. There'd been no change. They were as close as ever, apparently, the lawman's friendship usurping her place with him. When she'd learned he'd gone to Colorado, there had

107

existed the hope they'd come to a parting of the ways, which was what should happen. How could there exist a sincere friendship between a stiff-necked lawman and a notorious outlaw? It didn't make sense.

"Seems there was a bunch of them wild Texas cowhands celebrating the end of a cattle drive. Was really tearing up the town, shooting, yelling, cussing, scaring folks they run into.

"Earp's been a great one to enforce the town ordinance about carrying firearms, so he headed up the street to put a stop to all the tomfoolery. He made a beeline for the Long Branch where he had a double-barreled shotgun stashed but before he got there he run smack-dab into a couple of them in the alley."

Kate listened absently, caring little for the recounting but waiting eagerly for the part where Doc had apparently taken a hand.

"Happens they knew him and he knew them. He'd had trouble with them before somewheres else and when they spotted him they had their guns out and were taking pot shots at the signs along the way. Earp was caught flat-footed, his pistols still in their holsters."

It would have solved a big problem for her if they'd used them on him instead of the signs, Kate thought.

"One of them yelled, 'We're going to kill you, Earp!' and I reckon as how they would've, only Doc Holliday was inside the Long Branch, right near the back door. He jumped up, grabbed a pistol out of a holster hanging on a peg, and drew his own. It's a big, nickel-plated .45—"

"I know," Kate murmured.

Doc had replaced the weapon he'd lost to the

marshal that night in The Flat soon after they settled in Dodge. A traveling gun peddler had come through town one day and he had traded the old cedar-handled pistol she'd gotten from the hostler for one more suited to his taste.

"Well, he stepped right out into the alley, cool as a cucumber. The rest of that bunch of trail hands had showed up by then. There must've been at least twenty of them, maybe more. But that didn't cause Holliday to back up one step.

"The two who'd first jumped Earp were cussing at him, trying to rag him into going for his gun but the marshal wasn't back of the barn when the brains was passed out. He knew damn well he didn't stand a chance against a bunch of crazy drunks like them Texans so he just kept his mouth shut and his hands a long way from his pistols while he tried to ease closer to the back door of the Long Branch.

"About that time that Doc Holliday stepped out into the alley and hollered at them cowhands to throw down their guns. Guess it surprised Earp as much as it did them but he didn't waste no time looking to see who it was. Said later he didn't have to. Holliday's got a real thick Southern accent, you know."

Kate nodded. She liked to hear Doc talk, and once she'd sent him into gales of laughter when she'd asked him in all seriousness if the alphabet taught in the schools of the South where he was educated lacked the letter *r*.

"Anyways, when them drunks looked away, Earp drew both his guns and the whole thing was turned around mighty fast with him and Doc both holding guns in each hand and pointing them at them cowhands.

"Doc said, 'What'll we do with them, Wyatt?' and the marshal said, 'Cold-cock the lot. I'll start with this one' and then he steps up to the jasper who's been doing a lot of big talking, buffaloed him alongside the head with one of them long-barreled six-shooters of his, and laid him out flat.

"The rest was ready to call it quits right then and started dropping their guns. Was one, however, with just enough rotgut in him to be brave, and instead of doing like the others, he threw hisself down on Earp. Doc hollered at the marshal to look out and fired fast. Now, Doc ain't one to shoot a man just to teach him a lesson. When he throws down on a fellow he aims to kill him but this time his eye was off a mite and he only winged that dockwalloper in the shoulder.

"But it settled them Texans for sure and he and the marshal marched the whole push off to the calaboose and locked them up. Earp said later if it hadn't been for Doc Holliday he'd be dead, because that bunch was out to kill him for what he'd done to them before. Some of them was holding a grudge from the time when Earp was a deputy here in Wichita."

Kate sighed quietly. The tie between Doc and Wyatt Earp would be stronger than ever now, and she was practical-minded enough to know that she could never break it. Now that, added to the earlier acceptance of the fact that Doc was not setting out to find her, had brought their relationship into painful focus; she meant far less to him than he did to her, and his efforts to give her the life of respectability she'd thought she wanted had been done out of a sense of gratitude for that night in The Flat when she had saved him from a lynch mob.

110

That the experiment in gentility had failed was no fault of his, only hers, and whether he would have eventually weakened and returned to the old way of living was problematical, a question that now could never be answered. Regardless, it was he who counted with her; she'd take him on his own terms—for a half a life with him was better than what she had now.

By morning Big Nose Kate was on her way back to Dodge City.

15

Holliday was sitting at a table in the rear of the Long Branch when she walked in. The bar was crowded but there were no card games in progress, and alone, he was idly shuffling a deck of cards between his long fingers. He looked tired, she thought, probably was neglecting himself more than ever. When they were living together she did see to it that he ate fairly regularly and got a little sleep.

"Hello, Doc—"

He raised his eyes to her. They seemed bluer than she remembered, with a brightness that could be caused by fever. The familiar, twisted smile pulled at his lips.

"Kate."

She moved to the table, sat down, not certain if he was pleased to see her or not. "Been quite a spell," she murmured.

"Has at that. Seven months, thereabouts."

She felt her spirits lift. He had taken note of the

time she'd been away. It could mean that he had actually missed her.

"Was in Wichita."

"Heard that. Town's pretty tame, they say."

"Not just tame—dead. Things still going good here in Dodge, I expect."

"Are for a fact," he replied, expertly maneuvering the deck of cards he was toying with. "Biggest summer they've seen yet. More trail drives coming into here than anybody can remember. Place is boiling with cowhands."

"You doing all right—not sick or anything?"

His slight shoulders stirred beneath the coat he wore. Elsewhere in the saloon, conversation was a steady drumming sound, interrupted now and then by a shout or a burst of laughter. Someone was at the piano picking out a tune with one finger.

"I'm fine," he said.

Abruptly Kate was fed up with the fencing, the pointless chitchat. "Oh, the hell with all this," she exclaimed with a nervous laugh, "I've missed you to beat the devil, Doc. Kept hoping you'd miss me enough to come after me, drag me back by my hair, but you never did."

"Was your choice," he said but there was a softness to his drawling words.

"I know that, and I was dead wrong. Was me that threw the best kind of life I ever had, away. I guess it was that Wyatt Earp showing up right when he did that set me off and—"

"No reason for you to feel the way you do about him."

"I keep telling myself that, but it's still there. I

114

can't help it. I guess I'm just jealous of him, of your friendship."

Holliday laid the cards on the table in a neatly squared stack, and taking out his handkerchief, coughed into it.

"That's plain silly, Kate," he said after he had regained his composure. "Wyatt's just a friend, and I enjoy talking to him. He's an educated man and it's a relief to be around him and pass the time after having to put up with the usual run of cowhands, stinking buffalo hunters and such that I'm up against the majority of the time."

She smiled faintly. "That list include me?"

"Hardly. Wyatt gives me one thing, you another. There's no connection."

Kate was quiet for a long breath, then: "You willing for us to go back living together?"

"Sure. Why not? Truth is, Kate, I'd like it. Might as well own up to it—I've missed you."

That was all she wanted to hear—that, and his stated desire to resume their relationship as man and wife.

"I'll go out and scout us up a place to live," she said happily, coming to her feet.

He stayed her with an outstretched hand. "No need, I've got a house down the street a ways," he said, rising. "Not much, but it's comfortable, and it's a fair piece from all the racket that's going on day and night. Can sleep without some wild yahoo waking you up every ten minutes. I'll show you . . ."

Taking her bag, he led the way through the saloon, coolly staring at the men who paid undue attention to Kate. Once outside, shouldering a path through the steady flow of pedestrians on the walk, he glanced at her. She was smiling, aware of the attention she had drawn. Abruptly he stepped into a passageway between two adjacent buildings and drew her after him out of the traffic.

"Best we settle this before we go any farther," he said, his features stern. "Around here you're still known as my wife. Maybe it's unfortunate but we started it and we'll have to stick to it."

"Of course."

"And you'll live up to it! I won't have you laying with every young stud that comes along and takes your fancy."

"I don't intend to," Kate said.

"What's more, you'll work in the Long Branch where I'll be."

A spark had sprung to life in Kate's eyes. Getting together again was one thing, but having the law laid down to her as if she were a child was something else.

"What difference will it make whether I'm working in the Long Branch or the Alhambra or one of the other saloons? They're all the same."

"Makes plenty to me. If I have to kill a man over you then I want whatever happened to cause it to be firsthand, not some tale somebody brings to me."

"Which all boils down to one thing—you don't trust me."

"Exactly what I mean," Holliday said flatly and took a drink from a bottle he was carrying in his pocket.

A slow smile parted her lips. "Always hoped you'd be a bit jealous."

"Not that at all," he snapped. "You're playing the part of my wife. Aim to see that you act it out right."

Kate shrugged wearily and they moved on. Coming

116

to a cross street, they turned into it, and a block or so down its dusty length, Doc cut into the weedy yard of a small cottage. It was badly weathered and showed neglect. Her skeptical appraisal was not lost on him.

"I said it wasn't much, but it's quiet. Expect you can see that."

"It'll do fine," Kate replied, again happy, and followed him into the low-roofed structure.

"Maybe we can find something better before winter sets in."

Halting in the center of the room that served as a parlor, she gazed about and shook her head. "A good cleaning would help a lot."

"Plenty of time later for that," Holliday said, pointing. "The bed's in there."

As Doc had told her, Dodge City was fairly overflowing with cowboys and each night the Long Branch, as well as the innumerable other saloons, was packed with laughing, shouting, shoving men, all struggling to find a place at the bar, or dance with one of the dozen or so girls there for the purpose.

Kate, with the dullness of Wichita washed from her after a single hour that first night, was again the bright and happy woman of old, accepting favors, whirling with a partner to the thumped-out tune on the piano, and deftly turning aside all offers to retire to her room, her partner's quarters or anywhere else convenient.

Night after night the frolic held while Holliday worked at his game, most of the time a winner, occasionally the loser but on balance well ahead. It was the idyllic life again for Kate, the gay, busy hours until early morning, home then to the cottage with Doc,

117

and to bed; rising somewhere after noon, meals at Delmonico's or one of the newer restaurants that had come into being during her absence, and then again to the convivial Long Branch to resume the heady routine when the shadows began to lengthen.

It worked well. She saw Wyatt Earp only occasionally since his duties as the town's deputy marshal demanded most of his time, and recalling the distinction Doc had expressed as to their relation to him, she made an effort to be polite if not cordial. The lawman viewed her in much the same light, and so between them there sprang up a sort of tremulous truce.

The first rent in the quietly billowing canvas appeared one evening a few weeks after her return to Dodge City. Since the incident in which Holliday had stepped in to save his life at the hands of the cowboy gang, Earp had conferred upon him the unofficial status of deputy. Once or twice he had called on Doc to assist him in making an arrest, a matter involving only a few minutes of time.

In this case, however, it meant being gone from town for the night and possibly all of the next day.

"You're no lawman!" Kate stormed when Holliday informed her that he was going. "I won't have you playacting one! You could get yourself shot."

"Wyatt needs my help," he replied, and thus settling the argument, rode off with the marshal.

Kate sulked. It was their first hard quarrel since getting back together, and, she realized bitterly, it was over Wyatt Earp. Doc knew how she felt about the lawman, that she didn't trust him, resented him, even feared what he might one day do to Doc, who after all was as much an outlaw as the renegades they went after. But how she felt made no difference to him; all right, how *he* felt sure as hell shouldn't make any difference to her. She'd do as she pleased, just as he did.

That night, whirling about the dance floor to the lively music, with several drinks too many under her bright green dress, she succumbed to the persistent proposals of a handsome young cowhand from Texas and ended up spending the early hours in his hotel room.

The slam of the cottage door around noon that following day awoke her with a start. She sat up, suddenly afraid. It was Holliday. He had returned from his trip with Earp and, from the hard set of his features, had learned of her escapade with the cowboy.

For a long minute he simply stared at her, and then wheeling, snatched up his carpetbag, jerked it open and began to cram pieces of clothing into it.

Kate rose hurriedly. "Doc, I—I—"

"Forget it!" he snarled. "Heard all about you and that goddamn saddle-tramp. By noon it'll be all over town. My wife laying up with—"

"Wouldn't've happened if you hadn't gone off with Earp!" Kate shouted, her temper flaring.

"That oughtn't to make any difference!"

"No, of course not, not as long as it's what you wanted! What I want never counts!"

"Well, you've got your way now," he snapped. "Do whatever you damn please. I'm pulling out, and long as you're here in Dodge, I won't come back."

"Good!" Kate screamed, snatching up a half-filled bottle of whiskey and hurling it at him. "Long as I'm here I don't want you back!"

Holliday, oaths crackling from his lips, dodged the

119

bottle, allowing it to smash against the wall. Pivoting, he jerked the door open.

"You can depend on that!" he said in a savage tone and stepped out into the yard.

Kate stared through the doorway into the weed-overgrown yard for a long minute, and then, rising, she crossed and slammed the panel shut.

"The hell with you, Doc Holliday!" she shouted after his unseen figure.

16

The comparative doldrums that came with the advent of winter to Dodge City that year were less noticeable to Kate than usual, despite the absence of Doc, who, she steadfastly assured herself, was out of her life forever.

Soldiers were plentiful, having been brought in to help cope with a sudden surge of Indian trouble, and the town was still well populated by cowboys, who were laying over in anticipation of a big cattle drive that was to get underway in the spring along the Western Trail.

There had been but one adjustment in her style of living; she had moved out of the cottage once occupied by her and Doc and into one behind the Western Hotel. It was more to her liking since it offered better conveniences, complete privacy and contained no disturbing memories of the past.

She pursued her profession with joy and abandon. Gay, physically attractive and no longer one of the calico girls, she dressed in silks and satins and was constantly in demand. The hesitancy on the part of those who were aware of her relationship with Doc was dispelled by the end of the first week or so; to those newcomers who asked timorously if she were not the wife of the feared gambler and gunman, she would assure them with a shrug and say, "I was—once," and the element of danger was dispelled.

Gunshots awoke her early one morning in October, and joining the quickly assembling crowd at one of the cabins a short distance below hers, she was startled to learn that one of the saloon girls, a part-time actress, Dora Hand, had been murdered.

A Texan by the name of Spike Kennedy was the man who had committed the crime, she heard Wyatt Earp tell the deputy who had come with him to investigate the shots. She still had no use for the tall lawman, but like most everyone else in Dodge, she was forced to admit that he was making law and order mean something in the settlement. Why, it was said that more than four hundred dollars worth of Bibles had been sold that year!

Kate retraced her steps to her lodgings, turning aside a would-be client who spotted her in the crowd, and climbed back into bed. Had Doc been there, he would have been Earp's right-hand man in the lining up of a posse and going in pursuit of Spike Kennedy; stalking about, giving orders, his face set to stern, hard-case lines, he would be like a small boy showing off in front of company, which was exactly the effect Wyatt Earp seemed to have on him.

Doc, so she'd heard, was somewhere in Colorado again, and there was a rumor that the Santa Fe Railroad was heading into an all-out battle with the Denver and Rio Grande line for track rights through the mountains and was recruiting a company of gunmen to clear the way for them. Doc was among those being hired.

It sounded like him. He'd want to be right in the thick of it, curses on his lips, a bottle of whiskey in his left hand, that nickle-plated .45 in his right. He'd killed a couple of men since he rode out of Dodge, it was said, and being a gunfighter for the railroad would be to his liking.

She stood that winter's night at the bar in Dog Kelley's Alhambra, which was enjoying an unusual surge of business from the publicity arising over Dora Hand's killing. She looked pensively out over the crowd. The saloon was packed. The voices of the dealers at the gambling devices as they called out the odds, were loud and overrode the steady rumble of all else in the room. The dance floor was packed and the side boxes were filled. She, alone, appeared to be the only person in the place not enjoying herself.

"You got troubles, dearie?"

Kate turned to the woman at her side. She was the one they called Marcie, married to a worthless sort of man who did odd jobs around town when he was sober.

"No more than you."

Marcie smiled tiredly. "Going to quit this job if my old man ever gets squared around," she said. "May anyway if he don't. Just pull up and leave."

Kate eyed her sympathetically. "You're hoeing a hard row, all right, but you won't leave him. Women are all a bunch of damned fools—suckers. We get a man under our skin and no matter what kind of a son of a bitch he is, we can't turn loose."

"Not me!" Marcie said firmly. "You give me the chance and I'm gone!"

"What I thought, once," Kate replied. "Goddamn them. I'm finding out you can't live with them and you can't live without them!"

Marcie grinned and waved off a soldier weaving unsteadily toward her. "You talking about Doc?"

Kate shook her head angrily, denying the truth. "Talking about all of them."

Marcie studied her for a time, smiled again, and then nodding to the soldier, permitted him to draw her off toward the dance floor.

"Just fooling myself," Kate thought as the two disappeared into the shifting, swirling crowd. "I miss Doc, goddamn him! I wish he was here and we were living together like before. He's no good. He's mean and he's impossible to be around for more than an hour at a time, and one of these fine days he's going to get his fool head shot off, but it doesn't make any difference. I miss him like hell."

But she'd be damned if she'd go chasing after him. He'd walked out on her, and by God, he'd have to do the coming back. It was his move. She'd swallowed her pride and done the crawling after Wichita, hadn't she? Well, it was his turn now. She'd stand pat, leave it up to him this time.

"Going to be all hell busting loose come good weather. Ain't nothing stopping the Santa Fe."

Kate turned to the man moving up beside her. He made a gesture to the friend with whom he'd been speaking and who was now moving off, and grinned at her.

"Buy you a drink, lady?" he asked, looking her up and down with appreciative eyes.

124

"Sure, why not. What's your name, mister?"

"Abel Larkin. Folks that know me call me Abe. You're Kate. Bartender—whiskey down here."

Noah Converse, one of the men behind the busy counter, hurried up, refilled Kate's glass from one bottle, and with expert sleight-of-hand, used a different one for Larkin. Collecting the coins laid out before him, he pulled quickly away in response to another summons.

"You're new around here," Kate said, touching her glass to his, and then tossing off the drink in a single gulp.

"Yeah, sort of come and go. Work for the Santa Fe."

"Heard what you said about it. There really going to be trouble between the two companies?"

"Unless the Denver and Rio Grande backs off. We're set to go through the Arkansas Canyon, maybe over Raton Pass, too. Nothing's going to stop the Santa Fe."

"Even if it takes gunmen, killings—"

"You bet!" Larkin said, beckoning to Converse again. "That's how the Santa Fe gets things done —do whatever's necessary. They've put Cap Webb in charge of the brigade, and they don't come any better'n him when it's trouble you're facing. Saw your man with him a couple of weeks ago."

Kate's eyes narrowed. "My man—you talking about Doc Holliday?"

"Right! Want to tell you he's about the coolest customer I've ever come across. And cuss? Why, that man uses words I've never even heard of, some of them so strong they could whittle a tree down to a stump!"

125

Kate closed her eyes. Hearing news of Doc sent a warm flow coursing through her, but at once she cut it dead.

"Can think of better things to do than standing here yammering about him," she said indifferently.

Larkin swallowed his drink hastily and set the glass back on the counter. "Me, too! You got a place where we can go?"

Kate smiled, jerked her head at the bartender. "Just get a quart of whiskey and follow me," she said.

Abe Larkin dropped by again in midsummer. The anticipated war between the railroads had not materialized, he told her.

"Actually, we pulled a slicker on the Denver and Rio Grande. While they was digging in to hold the canyon, we snuck off and rammed our rails down through Raton Pass into New Mexico. The old Santa Fe's headed south and going full blast."

"There wasn't any shooting?"

"Nope. Sort of got a hunch that was all a cover-up."

Doc would have been disappointed, Kate realized, but he would be making the best of it where ever he was. That was one of the good things about him; he could fit himself in no matter the circumstances, and before you knew it, he would be prospering mightily.

"Seen Holliday in Las Vegas."

"Las Vegas—where's that?"

"Town in New Mexico. Railroad got there in June and him right with it. Somebody said he'd opened up an office of some kind. Dentist, I think it is. Sure didn't know he was a real doctor. Did you?"

Kate nodded. So it was Dr. John H. Holliday once

more, respectable, one of the accepted and undoubtedly well-thought-of citizens in a town where he was not well known.

"Could just be talk," Larkin continued. "When I saw him he was dealing faro in a saloon—his saloon, I was told. Makes more sense. Kind of hard to think a killer like him could be a dentist."

"He's done it before," Kate said abruptly. "Not much he can't or won't do when he sets his mind to it."

The urge to see Doc, to be with him again was hammering away inside her. He was starting off fresh and clean in a new town and she wanted to be a part of it. All her good resolutions to forget him, to leave it up to him to return to her, evaporated in a sudden gust of loneliness and desire.

"What was the name of that town?"

"Las Vegas."

"Can you get me on a train for there?"

Larkin stared at her, perplexed. "Yeh, reckon so. They're hauling passengers along with freight. You really want to go?"

"Just as soon as you can get me a ticket," Kate said.

17

"You know where I can find Doc Holliday?" Kate asked, climbing into the hack she found drawn up near the wooden structure that served as a depot in the new town of Las Vegas.

It was hot and the dust stirred up by the hundreds of people, horses and rigs crowding the street of the booming settlement was a choking cloud hovering over all.

The driver, a thick-set, dark-faced man with a stained and drooping mustache, bobbed his head. "Sure do," he said, considering her with interest. "Saloon ain't far from here. Climb in."

Settling herself on the grit-covered seat, Kate sighed resignedly. Wanting to look her best when she met Holliday, she had bought herself a stylish new outfit, a pale green affair with a flowing skirt and tight bodice that more than did justice to her figure.

But now, after the lengthy ride from Dodge in a converted railroad car more suited to gandy dancers and their like, and the encounter she was having with layer upon layer of Las Vegas' swirling, tan dust, she guessed her appearance would fall far short of the intended vision.

"I thought he'd opened up a dentist's office," she said, by way of gaining information.

"Did, but seems he don't pay much attention to it anymore," the driver said as he wheeled the surrey about. "Reckon he's doing too good in the saloon business. Was talking to Bill Leonard the other day and he said Doc hadn't been around in weeks."

Kate brushed at her face with a lace handkerchief and let her glance drift over the crowds jamming the street. Boom towns were always the same—dirt, shacks and anxious-looking people in a hurry.

"Who's Bill Leonard?" she asked.

"Jewelry store man. Got his place next to Doc Holliday's office over in Old Town. Sort of good friends, I think."

Just *sort of* would be putting it correctly, she thought, unless Doc had changed. He was a man who never took anyone to himself closer than arm's length.

"Old Town?'

"Yeah. This here's what we call New Town. Old Town's over there," the driver said pointing to the west where there appeared to be trees and more buildings. "The railroad missed it. Doc's office is down there, got his saloon here. That's it on ahead."

Kate leaned forward and viewed the unpainted, false-fronted structure toward which the driver guided his hack. It was mid-afternoon and a steady din was pouring from its open doorway. Business was better than good, she judged.

Waiting until the rig had halted, she tossed a silver dollar to the driver, thanked him, and then, suitcase in hand stepped down. Picking up her skirts, she waded through the ankle-deep loose dust to the saloon's entrance and paused.

The place was small, crude, choked with smoke and packed to capacity with men. She could see three or four women moving about and there were two bartenders behind the plank counter working steadily to satisfy the demands of patrons.

A few moments later she located Holliday and felt a tenseness grip her. He was standing back of the blackjack dealer, shoulders against the wall, hat tipped forward over his eyes, a cigar between his teeth. Arms folded across his chest, he was watching the play before him. There was a brownness to his usually pallid features and he looked younger, somehow.

Setting her bag behind the bar, she pushed her way through the crush and approached him from the side. He did not notice her presence.

"Doc," she said in a tentative voice.

He turned lazily to her. His lips parted, his brows came up reflecting brief surprise, and then he shrugged.

"What brings you here?"

His voice was cool, flat. Kate smiled. "You," she said frankly.

Holliday shook his head. "Afraid it was a waste of your time," he said, and beckoning, led the way to a small room in the rear of the saloon.

It was empty, filled only with the smell of stale tobacco smoke and spilled whiskey. It was furnished with a table and a half a dozen chairs and was evidently used for high-stake poker games. Settling down on one of the chairs and pulling a pint bottle of liquor from the pocket of his knee-length coat, Doc motioned for her to be seated.

Temper rising slightly at the chilly reception she was being accorded, Kate took a place opposite him. She reached for the bottle, pulled the cork and helped herself to a drink. He studied her through shuttered eyes.

"How're things in Dodge?"

"Slowing down."

"All the cowboys pull out?" he asked slyly.

"No, still plenty around. I see you've got yourself a few girls."

"Business, nothing more," he said crisply.

"Sure, sure," Kate murmured. They hadn't been together five minutes and already were beginning to quarrel. Resolutely she brushed it all aside.

"Good to see you again," she said with a broad smile. "Heard you were doing real good, that you'd even opened up your dentist's office again."

"Got it started but I haven't had much time for it lately. Money's in gambling, same as always. It's taken me a long time to get that through my head."

"You probably knew that all along, just didn't want to quit being a doctor."

Holliday smiled faintly. "Hell, you know better than that, Kate. I start practicing dentistry when I'm broke and need cash. That's all it's ever meant to me."

She watched him take a drink from the bottle. Then, "Where we staying?"

It was a carefully calculated question, one that went straight to the heart of the matter, as far as she was concerned.

He gave it thought, finally said, "Exchange Hotel. Got rooms there."

Kate sighed inwardly. She had been afraid of what his reply would be, but it had been as she hoped; he was agreeable to their living together again.

"Let's get one thing straight now," he said, muffling a cough with a cupped hand. "Forget this Mrs. Holliday thing. I won't having you shame me here in front of the people I know, like you did in Dodge. Call yourself whatever you like as long as it isn't Mrs. Holliday."

"I stopped doing that a long time ago in Dodge," she said and paused.

Some sort of disturbance had arisen in the saloon. Voices were shouting, a chair or a table crashed. Doc rose, stepped to the door, opened it and looked into the room. Beyond him Kate could see men thrashing about, knocking furniture in all directions as they fought among themselves. She smiled contentedly; it was like the earlier days in Dodge, before Wyatt Earp came along to put a damper on everything.

The racket lessened, ceased. Doc, going through another coughing spell, remained for a few moments at the door, and then closed it and returned to his chair. He hadn't asked about Earp yet, Kate realized; she was hoping he would not.

"Chance to get rich here," he said, downing a swallow of whiskey. "Town's gone crazy with the railroad coming here and all that. Going to be sort of headquarters as they work south. Give me a year and I'll have enough cash to call it quits."

He'd never do that. Kate had seen too many gamblers in her time and knew it was not in them to ever lay down the cards. Gambling was a disease, a virulent, tenacious malady and once it invaded a man's blood he could never rid himself of it.

133

But she said, "Sounds great, Doc. Then you could move to where ever it is folks go to cure a cough."

"Guess maybe I could at that," he agreed. "The both of us. Come on, I'll take you to the hotel."

Kate, pleased at his words, rose and they returned to the main part of the saloon. Pausing at the bar to retrieve her bag and for Doc to give instructions of some sort to one of the men working behind it, they moved on out onto the street.

At the hotel he escorted her to his quarters, two spacious rooms in the upper front of the hotel that overlooked the turbulent scene below. He helped her to get settled. Afterwards it was like the times in The Flat and Dodge and Kate reveled once again in the pleasures of being his woman.

"Going to be good having you around," he said as he sat at the window looking out. "Can be like this long as you behave."

"Long as it's like this I'll have no reason not to."

She might have also said there'd be no problems in the future as far as she was concerned if Wyatt Earp or someone like him didn't appear and start hanging about and claiming his attention, but she wisely let it pass.

Maybe there was a future for them—maybe they'd hit upon the opportunity that everyone hoped to find, that bonanza where you hit it big and were then able to slip away and live a life of luxury and contentment. With her help Doc might be able to give up gambling to some extent—at least the big high-roller sessions. It would be nice to have a quiet, little home in some out-of-the-way town where they could be just another married couple living out their lives in dull routine.

Doc would be different then, she was sure. Ordinarily he was about as affectionate as a diamondback rattlesnake, but there were exceptions when he displayed moments of tenderness, and it just could be that under more domestic conditions the inborn gentleman in him would surface more frequently and he would become like any other loving husband. Kate, sitting on the edge of the bed, clad in her new yellow silk dressing gown, studied him thoughtfully.

He did look better. The tan he'd acquired while working and living outdoors during his railroad employment, had benefited him considerably. His face was less haggard, his cheek bones not so prominent; only his eyes were the same, that clear, blue brilliance that seemed to arise from some deep-seated fire.

A sudden hammering on the door jarred her to reality. She glanced up. Holliday, reacting coolly, drew his pistol and stepped into the adjoining room.

"Who is it?"

"Leonard—"

Leonard. She recalled hearing the hack driver mention the name along with the information that he owned a store next to Doc's office. The key grated in the lock and she caught the thump of boots as the man came into the room.

"What's the matter?"

"They're coming for you, Doc," Leonard said, sucking hard for breath. "You've got to get out of here fast!"

Kate sprang to her feet and hurried to the archway that separated the two rooms where she could hear better. A heaviness was filling her. Doc was in some sort of trouble.

"Who's coming for me?"

135

Holliday voiced the question in his easy, drawling way that was characteristic when he was under stress.

"That bunch that calls themselves the Law and Order Committee. Aim to arrest you for killing Gordon."

"Arrest me! Goddammit to hell, they ought to give me a medal for blasting that son of a bitch!"

"Know that, but they're out to clean up the town and make it a decent place to live in, so they say."

Bill Leonard was a tall man with a cropped beard and a flowing mustache. He started for the window to have a look at the street below, saw Kate and pulled up short.

"Oh, hell—I'm sorry—"

Doc nodded. "It's all right. She's an old friend from Dodge. Name's Kate Elder. Kate," he added, gesturing at the jewelry store owner, "like for you to meet Bill Leonard, sort of a business associate."

Leonard hastily acknowledged the introduction and continued on to the window. "Not in sight yet. They went to the saloon first. Somebody heard you telling Aikens you'd be here, and told them. I beat it out the back so's I could get here and warn you. You'd best pull freight, Doc. They sure mean to hang you!"

Holliday swore deeply, wheeled, and stepping into the bedroom, angrily began to throw his belongings into a carpetbag. She noticed it was the same one he'd been carrying that day when he'd arrived in The Flat.

"Leaving the place to you, Kate," he said, drawing on his coat. "Keep it, sell it, do whatever the hell you like. Luck's just plain run out on me, seems."

Leonard pausing in the doorway, cut in anxiously. "Doc, there ain't no time left. Come down the alley. I'll have your horse standing ready."

He didn't wait for an answer and rushed out. Kate,

136

spirits falling lower with each fleeeting moment, sank onto a chair.

"Where'll you go?'

He gave that brief thought. "Dodge, I reckon. Can't think of any other place."

"I'll come as soon as I can."

He frowned and she knew he was remembering his vow to never again return while she was there. But he did not mention it and shortly he straightened up, packed and ready to leave.

"Suit yourself," he said, and started across the room. "You need any help with the saloon, talk to Aikens. He's my head barkeep. He'll know what's best to do."

Abruptly he halted. The sound of loud voices came from the street in front of the hotel. A tight grin pulled at his mouth.

"The Law and Order Committee," he said grimly, and hurried on to the door.

Kate followed instantly. "Run, Doc. I'll keep them here long as I can!"

He bobbed his head and stepped out into the hall. Glancing back over his shoulder, he said, "So long, lady," and rushed on.

18

Kate locked the door and stood in silence, hearing the thud of Holliday's boot heels as he passed down the hallway to the stairs that led to the rear entrance of the hotel.

The babble of voices in the street had swelled to a higher volume but as she listened, the sound became muffled and she supposed the crowd was entering the building and moving toward the room where they expected to find Doc. Somehow she'd have to stall them, keep them there for as long as possible so that he could get well out of town.

A wryness born of frustration curled her lips. Doc spoke of his luck running out; hers was no better, she thought, and coming about, she examined her reflection in the wavy mirror of the dresser.

Her appearance could stand repair. Reaching into her bag, open on one of the straight-backed chairs, she found her cosmetics and applied rice powder and rouge to her skin and lips. That chore done hastily, she brushed back her hair with her hands and settled the dressing gown about her body. Almost immediately there was a scuffling noise in the hall and then a fist hammered on the door.

"Holliday—come out of there! We're wanting you for murder!"

"Don't try running!" a second voice advised. "We got men all around this place, and we're all armed."

"Holliday! You hear? We know you're in there!"

Kate moved up to the door, turned the key and stepped back. Doc had apparently gotten clear of the hotel before any of the committee had taken up places in the alley, so there was no worry there.

The panel swung in hard and banged back against the wall. Several men, pistols drawn, pushed in cautiously. A half a dozen more, equally ready, were out in the hall.

"Come in, gentlemen," Kate said, smiling.

The committee members halted abruptly at the sight of her. Several low whistles sounded and from the hallway someone softly cried, "Whoo-eee!"

The astonishment passed quickly. The two men in the forefront brushed past her, made a hasty investigation of the adjoining bedroom and then retraced their steps to where she stood in cool silence under the admiring stares of the party.

"Where is he? Where's Holliday?"

Kate's white shoulder stirred beneath the silken gown. "Gone. A long time ago."

The taller of the two leaders swore and looked more closely at her. "Don't recollect seeing you around before. Who are you?"

"Kate Elder. Just got in today from Dodge City. You, or any of you, want to see more of me I'll be at Doc's saloon. I'm taking it over."

140

A man in the hall yelled an approval which was quickly hushed when the committee chief threw an angry glance in his direction.

"Where'd Holliday go?"

"Who knows?" Kate said with a wave of disinterest. "Pueblo, I expect, or maybe Denver. Used to work up there. Could be going back."

"Well, he can't've got far," the man said. "Know damn well he was up here in this room a couple of hours ago."

Kate faced him squarely. "Well, he damn sure ain't here now," she said, mimicking his tone, and when the laughter had died, added, "Now the bunch of you get out of here so I can dress. Come by my place tonight and I'll treat you all to a drink."

Loud approval greeted the offer. The party shifted and began to move back into the hallway. Only the pair who appeared to be heading up the crowd held back.

Kate considered them stonily. "Well?"

The younger one shook his head and turned to his partner. "She's telling the truth. No reason for her not to."

"Unless she's Holliday's woman."

"She'd a gone with him then, was that the way of it. Smart thing for us to do is mount a posse, ride north."

The tall man nodded. "Yeh, reckon you're right," he said and, bowing slightly to Kate, said, "Sorry to've bothered you ma'am," and followed his partner out of the room.

She was Doc's woman, by God, and she should have gone with him, Kate thought, shutting the door and once again locking it. That was how it ought to

141

have been, like back in The Flat when they'd fled a vengeful posse and had a high old time of it in the doing. But here in Las Vegas things hadn't shaped up right, and although it had been up to her more or less to again save him from a rope, he had ridden off without her.

Sitting down on the edge of the bed, Kate went back over the last few minutes when she was with Doc, reviewing what had been said: she was to take over the saloon—he was returning to Dodge City. That was the gist of it.

The hell with that, she thought. Suddenly angry, she snatched up the empty whiskey bottle standing on the floor nearby and threw it against the wall. She wasn't about to get stuck with his goddamned saloon! If it didn't mean enough to him to keep it, it sure as the devil was even less important to her!

Let that bartender Aiken, or whatever his name was, or Bill Leonard take over. She wasn't about to hogtie herself down in a dump like Las Vegas, not while Doc was living it up big in Dodge.

But she would do this much for him, for old time's sake; she'd go down to the place, take charge and see that things were run right. It wouldn't be wise to climb onto the train and head out for Dodge just yet anyway. The Law and Order Committee could be keeping an eye on her. That one jasper, the tall one, didn't act as if he really bought her story about Doc lining out for Colorado, and with everybody getting so holy-joe-minded anymore, they might telegraph the Kansas authorities and put them on the watch for Doc.

There was no doubt in Kate's mind that, confronted with a writ or whatever it was that judges issued to permit a lawman from one state to arrest somebody in

142

another, Wyatt Earp would honor it and supposed friend or not, he'd grab Doc and hand him over to the committee for a trial and hanging without batting an eye.

She'd wait a few days, maybe even a couple of weeks, until she was sure there was no danger to Doc and then she'd pull out. Meanwhile she'd do what she could to sell the saloon while stashing away all the extra profit she could get her hands on to turn over to Doc when she rejoined him.

Being presented with a few thousand dollars should make him feel good, but she knew that wasn't necessarily true. Money was something he viewed with no particular feeling one way or the other; either you had it or you didn't and such status was of no consequence in his scheme of things.

She turned then to her clothing, dressed leisurely in one of her newer frocks, a black and gold spangled affair that came just below her knees and showed off her legs to good advantage. Then, pocketing her derringer in preference to the heavier belted gun, she went down to the street and engaged a hack to take her to the saloon.

She was expected and cheers went up as she walked in behind the counter and took a place between the two bartenders on duty.

"Are you Aiken?" she asked, singling out the man she'd noticed Doc speaking to.

He nodded, displaying no friendliness.

"I'm taking over here. You know about it?"

Aiken shrugged indifferently. "He told Bill Leonard to give me the word."

"Good, then you know," Kate said, facing the man squarely. "If you've got any objections, you're fired.

Goes for you, too," she continued, shifting her glance to the second bartender. "If not, stay on the job—same wages, same everything."

Several men at the bar, overhearing her straightforward ultimatum, laughed. Aiken reddened and swallowed noisily.

"Ain't sure I'm going to like working for a woman."

"Well, I'm a woman and now's the time to back off if that's how you feel. Expect I can find plenty who'll be glad to take on your job. Expect what you knock down on the side and what you get paid makes it a pretty good deal."

Aiken looked down and scuffed at the sawdust covered floor with the toe of his boot. "Hell, I don't do no knocking down—"

"Don't pony me, mister!" Kate snapped. "I've spent my life around places like this. I know what goes on. What's it to be?"

"Reckon I'll stay."

Kate glanced at the man beyond him. He nodded promptly.

"All right, it's settled. You do your jobs right and I'll see that Doc gets the word. Try crossing me and he'll hear about that mighty quick, too. Understand?"

"Yes'm," Aiken said meekly, turning to face the deep crowd pressing up to the bar. "Who's next?"

Kate moved across behind them, made her way into the pushing, shoving pack, expertly avoiding the eager hands reaching for her. She called the dealers together, found they had also been advised of Doc's wishes by Bill Leonard, and gave them their choice—stay or quit. All agreed to continue. She didn't bother to consult the women. They could do as they wished since replacements were always plentiful and she knew from experience that a change in faces was always good for business. Reliable barkeeps and straight dealers were a different matter, however.

The transition went off smoothly and for the first weeks the novelty of running a saloon intrigued her and left her with little time to think of anything else. But soon responsibility became boring and it was with a growing reluctance that she reported daily to the place.

She had retained Doc's quarters at the hotel for her own use and she began to spend more and more time in her rooms alone with no company other than a bottle. Finally she could stand it no longer; she was fed up to the gills with Las Vegas and the saloon, but mostly with the sort of life she was being compelled to lead, one wherein she looked on rather than participated in all the fun and frolic. And that deep-seated yearning for Doc was again stirring through her.

Making inquiries, she found that it would be possible to catch a train east that very night, one that would get her back to Dodge City. Accordingly she went into conference with Aiken, turned the operation of the firm over to him, and bought herself a ticket and packed her bag. By midnight Kate was on her way, dozing on an uncomfortable bench seat, refusing the invitatory glances turned to her by the assortment of drummers, soldiers, cattlemen, cowhands and the like who were fellow passengers.

The long, tiring journey punctuated by frequent jerky stops and starts and the monotonous clack of iron wheels meeting rail joints ended eventually, and once more she was walking along familiar streets pointing for the Long Branch where she could expect Doc Holliday to be.

Turning into the alley behind the saloon, she stepped up to the back door and entered. It was shortly past noon and there were only a few patrons at the bar. As she put her suitcase down in a corner she could not help noting the contrast between the dozing Long Branch and the saloon in Las Vegas where things would be going full tilt.

But that would change. Dodge had been a wild, roaring hell-bender of a town once, too. One day a Wyatt Earp would come along, and as he had done in Dodge City, clamp down hard, and Las Vegas would end up just like all the rest, just another stop along the line, another Wichita.

"Well, for lord's sake, if it ain't Big Nose Kate!"

She glanced up, glad to hear a friendly voice. It was Chalk Beeson.

"Good to see you back. Where you been?"

"Las Vegas, town at the end of the railroad. Doc around?"

"Holliday?" Beeson said, frowning. "No, he's been gone for quite a spell. Headed west out of here hoping to catch up with the Earps. They was going to Arizona."

19

"Arizona!" Kate echoed, disappointment overriding anger. "Expected to find him there."

Beeson looked at her curiously. "He tell you that?"

She shrugged. "No, not exactly. Far as he knew I'd be staying in Las Vegas. You say he went with Wyatt Earp?"

"Not at the start. Wyatt'd already quit his job and pulled out, him and his whole family."

"Family? Didn't know he was married."

"He ain't. By family I mean his brothers and their wives and kids. Wyatt's a widower. The whole push is moving to a town name of Tombstone. Big silver strike."

Kate, her spirits lagging, crossed slowly to the counter and motioned to Ernie the bartender to pour her a drink.

"So Doc threw in with him—them," she murmured, heavily.

Beeson nodded. "Yeah, but like I said, they'd already gone when he got here. He threw some grub in his saddlebags quick and took out after them. Like as not caught up with them somewheres this side of the Indian Territory. Know he did because there was a cattleman in here that seen them."

"Seen who?" Ernie asked, coming into the conversation.

"Kate here was asking about Doc Holliday and the Earp party."

The barkeep bobbed his head. "Last word I got was they'd crossed into New Mexico, was cutting across for Arizona. Indian trouble's keeping them to the north trail."

Nursing her drink, Kate stared moodily at her reflection in the back-bar mirror. Tombstone. A new town, wild and wide open from a silver boom. It would be a natural for Doc.

"You aim to go chasing after him?" Ernie asked.

The question roused her temper. "Why the hell should I? I don't need him!"

He had needed her though, once in The Flat, again in Las Vegas, not to mention that night on the trail to Dodge. Goddamn him, you'd think he'd show a little appreciation.

Beeson smiled knowingly and winked at Ernie. "I sort of figured you would. You and Doc kind of fit together. Thought he'd probably sent word for you to join up with him."

She snapped up the opening to save her pride. "He could have and I didn't get it. Town like Vegas. It's pretty much of a mess."

It was a comforting thought, although far-fetched. He could have gotten in touch if he'd wanted to, either by mail or by a passing friend, and he certainly could have left a message for her there at the Long Branch.

148

But in his hurry to throw in with Wyatt Earp he'd forgotten her entirely.

"It much of a trip to Tombstone, you think?" she wondered, surrendering to what she knew was inevitable.

"Plenty far but folks are heading that way every day," Beeson said.

"Stagecoach?'

"Only way unless you want to fork a horse and saddle or maybe use a buggy. You deciding to go?"

Her shoulders stirred. "Thinking about it. Can I catch the stage out of here?"

"Expect so," the saloonman replied in a doubtful tone. "Be one hell of a hard trip, Kate. You sure you want to make it?"

She turned, glanced about the room. "Change would sort of be nice," she said. "Didn't like Las Vegas, and Dodge is getting to be like Wichita. Be a lot of things going on in a new town like Tombstone."

And Doc would be glad to see her if for only one thing; under her skirt she was wearing a money belt with almost five thousand dollars in paper and gold in its pockets, cash she'd set aside from the profits of his saloon. Chances were he'd be needing a stake and that much cash would start him off pretty good.

"Don't suppose you know when the stage pulls out?" she continued, an eagerness to be on her way now beginning to grip her.

"Southbound's what you'll be wanting to take," Beeson answered. "As I recollect they've got one leaving here every day."

"But you sure don't want to keep riding it south," Ernie cautioned. "Apaches are raising hell down in that part of the country. You buy yourself a ticket that'll get you into the north end of Arizona, then cut south."

Kate turned, picked up her bag and started for the door. Reaching it, she paused and looked back at the two men.

"Obliged to you for all the favors you've done me. In case I don't ever see you again, I—"

"Hell, Kate, no use talking like that!" Chalk Beeson broke in. "I'll give you odds you'll be back here inside six months!"

She smiled. "Just never know. So long."

Stepping out onto the breakneck boardwalk, Kate hurried to the stagecoach office. There were two ways she could cover the journey, the agent informed her; take the train to a town at the end of the line called Las Vegas, and catch a stagecoach there. Or she could get the southbound coach, which would be leaving shortly, and if she didn't want to stay with the regular route which continued on past Santa Fe and down the Rio Grande Valley to Socorro, she could transfer at the old capital city to a coach that angled across the upper half of New Mexico and reached Arizona Territory from that point.

It was a mighty rough trip and there weren't any regular stage lines, only short, local outfits that connected the larger towns. She'd be taking a chance in some areas, might even have to hire a rig in order to get to a place where there'd be a stage stop. But others wanting to dodge the Indian trouble had done it and there was no reason why she couldn't.

Kate thanked him for his advice, purchased a ticket, and after strapping on her pistol, found herself a seat in the coach. For a time she was the sole passenger and then just before departure time two men climbed aboard and sat down opposite her. Both nodded pleasantly but confined their remarks to each other, and after they got off late the following day at a small town near the New Mexico border, she was again alone.

At Santa Fe, boiling with railroad fever, she changed to a different coach, which made a fast trip across a high plateau and then down into a lush, green valley neatly platted with farms and shaded by giant cottonwood trees.

Picking up two passengers, a rancher and his wife at Bernalillo, a settlement where they crossed the Rio Grande river, they whirled on westward, skirting a line of long-dead volcanoes, set apart from the rest of the land by an irregular circle of fence-like lava beds.

The rancher and his wife dropped off at a cross-roads settlement near a place called Fort Wingate, and then just short of the Arizona border, the stage line ended.

Kate spent two days there waiting for a ride on west, finally managed it by joining up with a party of Mormons searching for good farming country where they could establish a settlement. It was a slow, tedious ride in the back of a spring wagon but eventually it ended when they reached a town named Joseph City where she was able to again take a stage-coach on west.

But that run expired, too, in a small place nestled in high mountains. It was called, simply, The Forks.

"You're wanting to go to Tombstone," said the man who operated the livery stable with also doubled as the way station. And added, scratching at his beard, "Then you'd best head south on the Chino Valley road to Prescott. Ain't no sense in you going on west. This here Tombstone, it's way down close to the Mexican border."

By now weary of it all, Kate sighed deeply. "How do I get to Prescott? Is there a stage?"

"Sure!" the hostler said in a faintly offended voice. "It's the capital and there's reg'lar runs heading there twice a week."

That was welcome news. "When's the next one?"

"Tomorrow morning."

"How far is it?"

"Ain't no more'n fifty mile. Stage'll get you there by noon."

Since Prescott was the seat of territorial government, she should have no problem continuing on to Tombstone from there, Kate reasoned.

"Count me in as a passenger," she said, glancing about. "There a place I can put up for the night?"

Again there was a note of injury in the man's voice. "Of course there is! We've got a hotel right on down the street. Good meals and real clean rooms."

Kate thanked him, sought out the hostelry and registered in. It was no more than a large house with a half a dozen rooms, but as the livery stable owner had said, it was clean, the meals good, and for the first time in many days and nights she slept in a comfortable bed.

Late that next morning the coach rolled into Prescott, a quiet-looking little town set deep in the hills, and drew up before a hotel. There were five other passengers on the ride, two men and three women, all of whom carefully avoided her doing the entire trip and held back while she stepped out of the coach into the clear, cool sunshine.

As she turned to take her bag, being dug out of

152

the boot by the driver, a familiar figure lounging against the porch post of a saloon and gambling house directly across the street caught her attention. She drew up sharply, a gasp of surprise, and then of relief slipping from her lips.

It was Doc Holliday.

20

Holliday saw her at almost the same moment. He straightened, a look of incredulity crossing his narrow face. Suddenly he grinned, his broad, strong teeth showing up whitely beneath the mustache curving down over his mouth.

He was pleased to see her, possibly even glad, Kate thought, taking her bag and moving across the street toward him; or else—and the harsh truth stabbed deeply into her—or else Wyatt Earp wasn't with him. That was it. They had said Earp was going to Tombstone; for some reason Doc had chosen to remain in Prescott.

"Kate!" he shouted, extending both arms toward her. "Never expected to see you here!"

"Surprised to see you, too," she answered, lowering the suitcase and taking his hands. "Chalk said you were going to Tombstone with the Earps."

"Was where we were headed," he explained, taking up her bag. "Wyatt and I held over for a few days while the rest went on. I started hitting it big at faro so when Wyatt got the notion to pull out, I stayed. Man's a fool to walk out on his luck when it's running. Kate, I'm ahead close to forty thousand dollars right now and the cards are still falling right for me!"

She had figured it correctly—Wyatt Earp wasn't around. It should make her angry but it didn't. Seeing Doc again, and being with him, was all that mattered.

"I've got five thousand more for you that I brought from Las Vegas."

"Keep it," he said with a wave of his hand. "It's all yours for looking out for things up there. You sell the place?"

"No, left Aiken in charge. Told him you'd get in touch."

His steps slowed. She glanced up. They were turning into a yard at the back of which stood a house with a sign declaring "Rooms To Let" suspended from its eaves.

"Where I'm staying," Holliday said. "Can get you a room for yourself, or you can move in with me. Up to you."

"You know how I want it," Kate said. "Will it cause you any trouble?"

"In this dump? Hell, no!" Holliday said with a laugh, and opening the door, led the way across a sort of parlor to a hallway and his quarters, which were at its far end.

"It's right on the alley," he said. "Learned that's a good location. Makes it easy to slip out the back when you have to leave in a hurry, like in Vegas."

They entered his room, a fairly large area, scantily furnished with bed, two chairs, a wardrobe, table and dresser. He glanced at her questioningly.

156

"Not the Exchange Hotel, but if you want something better, I'll see what I can find."

"Nothing wrong with this," Kate replied, sinking into the rocker.

She watched him place her bag on the bed, cross to the window and, drawing the sun-bleached lace curtain aside, glance out. He had changed little since Las Vegas, his skin still wearing a healthy tan, his eyes the same burning blue. She watched him come about, always intrigued by his easy, off-hand movements, which seemed to go with his drawling manner of speaking.

"I went to Dodge looking for you," she said. "Expected to find you there. Sure bowled me over when Chalk said you'd lit out for Arizona with the Earps."

"Was a sudden notion. They'd gone when I got there and it struck me all at once that it was high time I was moving, too. Figured I was all washed up far as that part of the country was concerned and it'd be smart to find new diggings."

"You could've sent word to me, or left it with somebody at the Long Branch."

He raised his gaze to her. His lean features were set. "Now, Kate, there was no reason to do that. There's nothing but being friends between us—no strings, no tags, no holds. You can go your way anytime you please, same as I intend to go mine."

"There could be more."

"I don't want more!" he snapped. "I refuse to let it be that way, not ever, and you know goddamn well why!"

"That makes no difference to me, Doc. I've told you so several times."

"Besides, we've tried this being man and wife. It

157

didn't work, and it never will. Get that in your head, Kate."

She waited while he turned his head aside and coughed deeply. When it was over she said, "What, then, do you—"

"We're friends," he cut in, "nothing more, and it ends there. If you can't see it that way now's the time to do something about it."

"Move on?"

Holliday took a bottle from his coat pocket, soothed his throat with a long swallow. "Exactly. I hope you don't. I like your being around. You're good company and we can have us a hell of a big time together, but I won't make any promises or keep you here under false pretenses."

Kate shrugged and began to unbutton her dress. "Half a loaf's better than none," a voice within reminded her as her fingers sought out the concealed money belt, released its ties and drew it from around her body.

"It's all right with me, Doc," she said, tossing the belt to him.

He caught the band of soft leather, glanced at it and laid it on the bed. "That's yours. Told you to keep it and I meant it," he said, and then after a thoughtful pause, continued. "I wonder, Kate. You've changed a plenty since we first met in The Flat. I doubt you'll be satisfied."

"Any woman would want more—"

"We tried respectability in Dodge," he reminded her. "You got sick of it mighty fast."

She nodded. "I know, and it was all my fault the way it turned out. I only wish I had it to do over."

"Hindsight's always better," he said, taking another drink. "But there's no going back, not to anything. What's done is finished, whether we like it or not."

"I know," she said wearily, "and I'm ready to settle for the best I can get."

"Now you're talking sense! In this lousy life you can only play whatever cards are dealt you and the sooner you learn to accept that fact, the sooner you'll be at peace with yourself. Now, what's your pleasure? You hungry? Want to eat? How about a drink? Got plenty here in the room."

Kate laughed, reached for the bottle he extended to her and helped herself to a satisfying portion. Only a few times in the past had she seen him so light-hearted. She would like to think it was all due to her arrival, but more than likely it was because he was riding high on a big winning streak.

"What kind of a town is this?" she asked later, as they stretched out side by side, relaxing.

"Pretty fair. Lot of money around."

"How about the law?"

Holliday laughed. "The marshal won't much go for you walking the streets with a gun strapped around your middle, but he leaves things pretty much alone. Good folks here are so busy trying to keep Prescott the territorial capital they don't have time to think of anything else."

"We plan to stay or go on to Tombstone?"

"Like I said, a man's a fool to walk out when his luck's running good."

Kate sighed happily. At least, with no Wyatt Earp to draw him away, he would be hers for a while, maybe for all time. If things continued to go right for Doc there in Prescott there was a good possibility they could remain, make it their permanent home. With the big pile of cash he had accumulated and the five thousand he was insisting she keep as her own, they could open up a place.

"Doc—"

He reached for the bottle and drank deeply. It stirred a brief spasm of coughing and he tipped the liquor to his mouth again to ease the irritation. It did not help, Kate knew, but he seemed to think it did, and his drinking was one thing she never questioned him about.

"Yeah?"

"Was just thinking: with all the money we've got, why don't we open up our own place? Then we could settle down here, make a home—"

"Dammit, Kate!" he broke in angrily. "What's it going to take to make you understand? I don't want that. I don't want anything—no tags, no strings— nothing! All I want is to live out what days I've got ahead and live them the way that pleases me most."

Kate was silent for a long minute after his outburst. "Was just a thought," she said, finally.

"Forget that kind of thinking. Just set your mind to having a good time and enjoying life. You're going to live only one time—even a dumb fool knows you ought to make the best of it. Let's go eat."

"Anything you say."

He sat up, swung his legs over the edge of bed, began to draw on his clothing. "There's a back room in one of the saloons where a woman's set up a place to eat. Not fancy like Delmonico's but the food is mighty tasty."

"Sounds good."

"It is. We'll eat, then go out front. No dance floor there, but you can pass the time at the bar or maybe

160

just stand by me. If my luck's not so good, I'll pick up and we can tour the rest of the joints like we did that first night in The Flat—" His words broke off. He looked back over his shoulder at her. "Down here, what do you want me to call you?"

"Kate Elder'll do."

He nodded and resumed his dressing. She rose, went to her suitcase, chose a somewhat conservative ensemble, a white silk shirtwaist, a pale blue pleated skirt with a matching bolero jacket. Somehow she didn't feel like wearing one of her customary gaudy affairs.

Finishing up with a touch of color on her cheeks and lips and a quick brushing of her thick, dark hair, she turned and found him studying her with distinct approval.

"By God, Kate," he said with a shake of his head, "you're a woman to turn Aphrodite green with envy! Come on, let's go. I want to show you off."

She didn't know who or what Aphrodite was, but she did recognize a compliment; she'd pleased him, and that was all that mattered.

The fall passed and the winter months, filled with gusty winds and snow flurries, began. As Doc wished, they lived a time of ease, enjoying the best with no thoughts of the future while they pursued his doctrine of taking life day by day and exacting the most from each one.

And then late in January, shortly after he had risen from bed and was shivering in the bitter cold that filled the room, a sudden wave of coughing assailed him, and left him head bowed, breathless and leaning

161

weakly against the wall. Kate, hastily bringing him a glass of water, looked on anxiously.

When he was again his normal self and the red flush had faded from his face, he turned to her. His eyes were unusually bright and there was a grayness to his lips.

"We're getting the hell out of this goddamn place," he said in an impatient, savage tone. "I can't live here."

She nodded. "Anything you say, Doc."

"Luck's changed, too. Back down to about forty thousand, and I won't dig into that."

"Where do you want to go?" She knew what his answer would be and dreaded it.

"Tombstone. Hear the climate's good and things are still going great."

Wyatt Earp would be there, too, Kate thought, bitterness stealing into her. "Isn't there some other town, maybe back in New Mexico? It's a good place for people with consumption."

"With that murder charge in Las Vegas still hanging over my head? No, can't do that. Only choice is Tombstone. Can you be ready by morning? I'll buy a rig and we'll head out then."

Kate turned away wearily. "I'll be ready," she said.

21

The change in Holliday was immediate. They checked into one of the hotels and before Kate had finished hanging their clothing in the closet, he had departed, stating his intention to look up Earp, who had assumed the job as a lawman of some sort.

It was difficult for her to understand the effect the man had on him. Ordinarily Doc was quiet, soft-spoken and intent to the point of seriousness; in the presence of Wyatt Earp he became a swaggering, blustering braggart seemingly bent on proving his reputation as a cold-blooded killer.

Time and again she'd endeavored to fathom the contradiction and always she had turned eventually away from the puzzle in a haze of frustration. Was it that the two men were so opposite—Doc, an acknowledged outlaw, notorious throughout the land, and Earp, a lawman of equal fame and stature? Did such contrast evoke a challenge within him?

Or did he derive a subconscious amusement from striding along the street, shoulder to shoulder with

Wyatt, peace officer and killer, one representing law and order, the other the exact opposite?

Doc apparently held some amount of fascination for Earp, too, else he would have admitted the incongruity of the friendship and long ago brought it to an end. It was a matter of faithful dog running with killer wolf, and Kate, while unaware of it, was not alone in her inability to comprehend the close companionship.

She could do nothing but give thanks for the intermittent periods during which Wyatt Earp had not been a factor in her relationship with Doc, and make the best she could of it when he was around. It was a conclusion born of practical wisdom, and finishing up the chore of arranging their few possessions, she went back to Fremont Street and began a leisurely stroll.

Tombstone was a lively place; miners, cowboys, drummers, gamblers, and well-dressed men who were probably mine owners or officials of some sort could be seen at every hand. Women were plentiful, too, and there was no lack of saloons and gambling halls, many with ornate, expensive-looking façades.

She did not encounter Holliday at once but she did see several familiar faces along the way. Among them was a girl she'd known in The Flat, who told her that business was good and if she wished to set up, there were plenty of beds available below Sixth Street.

"Doc and me are living at the hotel," she explained.

"Doc Holliday? You still with him?"

"Still," Kate replied, not bothering to reveal the irregularity of the arrangement.

"Well, if you ever decide to quit him, you know where to come," the woman said and moved on.

"Quit him!" Kate gave that some wry thought, wishing she might have the courage to do so. Actually it was the other way around. One day it would be Doc who left her and there was nothing she could do to forestall the probability, unless she put a bullet in Wyatt Earp's head. She smiled thinly at the idea. It was a good one but Doc would hate her for sure if ever she did. About all she could hope for along those lines was that Earp would die at the hand of some outlaw; then her problem would be solved.

She saw Doc at that moment. He had come out of a saloon called the Oriental and was standing with Earp and several other men on the walk. The lawman saw her and touched the brim of his hat.

"Big Nose Kate," he smiled. "I didn't know you'd hit town."

Holliday turned to him before she could reply. "Came in with me, Wyatt. We've got rooms at the hotel."

Earp's manner changed. "Didn't know, of course," he murmured, and nodding to her, added, "My brothers, Kate. Morgan and Virgil. The lady is Kate Elder, boys."

"And my woman," Doc stated with a wave of his hand.

She acknowledged the introductions to the Earps, neither of whom looked anything like Wyatt, she thought. All the while she was glowing from the flat declaration Doc had made as to her status. It could have been better only if he'd said she was his wife.

"Looking over the town?" Wyatt asked then, taking a thin, black cigar from his pocket and biting off the tip.

Virgil Earp dug into his vest pocket, produced a

match, and firing it with a thumbnail, held the flame to the weed.

"Busy place," Kate said, her eyes reaching beyond them to a tall, somber-faced man who pushed through the Oriental's doors and halted just outside. Decidedly handsome, he had dark, curly hair and the same icy blue eyes as Doc. He regarded her with frank interest.

"Reminds me of Dodge a long time ago," she finished.

"Be more money turned here than Dodge ever saw," Holliday commented, raising his glance to follow hers.

Virgil and Morgan Earp made no comment. It was apparent they didn't think much of her, or of Doc Holliday either.

The tall man was moving off. Doc nudged Wyatt, jerked a thumb at his receding figure. "Who's the well-heeled jasper with the two six-shooters?"

The lawman glanced over his shoulder. "Johnny Ringo," he said. "Don't ever sell him short. A hard one for sure and plenty fast with those guns."

"Just another four-flushing outlaw, far as I'm concerned," Morgan Earp said drily. "Hangs around with the Clantons and that bunch."

Doc's mouth pulled into a hard line. "You say the word, Wyatt, and I'll cut him down to size!"

"I've nothing on him," Earp cautioned. "So far he's clean. He ever stubs his toe, I'll take care of him."

Kate watched Ringo turn into another saloon. "Looks like a hell of a man to me," she said, smiling. "I want a drink, Doc. How about taking me inside and buying me one?"

He was staring at her, anger twitching his lips.

166

After a moment he said, "You go on. I've got business with Wyatt to take care of."

Abruptly he wheeled away, and in the company of the three Earp brothers he walked off down the street.

That, Kate soon realized, was to be the pattern of her life in Tombstone. They continued to live together in some sort of domesticity whenever he was not in the Oriental or the Alhambra or at one of the other saloons gambling.

During the day he was with Earp. Some sort of running feud had developed between the lawman and his followers, which included Doc, and the Clanton faction, who were lined up with the sheriff, John Behan. Ringo, who never failed to pause and courteously pass the time of day with her whenever they chanced to meet, was likewise a member of that party. Whatever the activity involved, Doc was continually being pressed into service as a deputy of Wyatt's.

Summer came, passed into fall and again it was winter. Kate still maintained their rooms in the hotel but Doc was seldom a visitor to them and she filled the day and night hours whiling away time in the various saloons, attending the Bird Cage Theater, and visiting with a woman named Nellie Cashman, with whom she'd become acquainted.

Doc was gone from Tombstone weeks on end, trying his hand at the games in Tucson, Bisbee and various other towns, or riding posse with the Earps, and by the time spring came again to the silver-loaded settlement in the gray-rocked Arizona hills, the static status of their relationship had grown into a chasm of considerable width.

Doc now spent all of his time, except when gambling, with Earp, doing his sleeping either at Wyatt's

167

house on First Street, or in the lawman's office. And there were other women in the picture. She took that discovery in stride and accordingly felt it her right to resume business operations. Since she was still a most attractive woman, her clientele grew quickly, embracing not only many of the town's more important men but the mysterious and handsome John Ringo as well, who, she learned, was the object of Doc's special hate for some unknown reason.

At the beginning she thought such action on her part might fan into life a spark of jealousy in Doc, particularly since Ringo was involved, but he passed it off, ignoring what undoubtedly had been called to his attention by the Earps as well as others.

"Knew her back in Dodge City," she heard him tell a man one night in the Alhambra as she sat at a table with a newcomer who had been drawn to her. "If he finds what he wants, good luck to him."

That officially sounded the death knell, insofar as their relationship was concerned. Doc had publicly renounced all claims to her and declared the field wide open, which indeed it had been for some months without proclamation.

Kate took it stoically. She rid herself of the newcomer, withdrew to a back corner with a bottle and proceeded to spend the night recalling the past with Doc, reliving all the good times as well as the bad.

She should not have expected more, she told herself over and over. Doc was the kind no woman could hope to hold. His attitude toward life was such that permanency was no part of his makeup in any way, and that with the insurmountable attraction and influence Wyatt Earp held for him, why, she was fortunate to have had his attention for as long as she did.

"You're looking like you've lost your last friend, Kate."

At the interruption of her morose thoughts, she glanced up. It was Mike Joyce, one of the town officials she'd met one night at Nellie Cashman's.

She nodded woodenly and he sat down at the table and helped himself to a drink from her bottle. Doc had gone on, she noted. He was probably with Earp. They were thicker than ever because of something to do with the political situation that had grown a bit tense since Tombstone had become the center of a newly created, important county in that part of the Territory.

"From what I heard Doc Holliday say, I reckon you and him are quits."

Kate nodded indifferently. She had drunk about half the quart of whiskey she'd begun with and it was having little effect. Of late it seemed to be taking more liquor than usual to put her in the right frame of mind.

"Yeh, we're quits—goddamn him!" she said, moved to sudden anger. "I hope him and that Wyatt Earp get their guts shot out."

Joyce smiled. "Pretty hard words."

"Mean them just the same."

"But you and Doc were friends for a long time—"

"Too long!" Kate said loudly, drawing herself up. "You want to dance with me?"

Joyce rose, kicked back his chair. "My pleasure to dance with a lady, anytime," he said gallantly, and reached for her hand.

169

22

Kate had never seen Doc in a worse mood, the depth of which was apparent to her even in her state of woozy intoxication. He had come to their rooms unexpectedly, entering the hotel by its rear door to avoid the excited crowds roaming the streets. There had been an attempted robbery of the Benson stage-coach, she'd heard, and there'd been some killing. Tombstone was up in arms over it.

She studied his angular shape, slumped deep in a rocker that stood in a dark corner of the front room. She felt much like a stranger and was not certain what to say. Shortly after arriving he had experienced a bad coughing spell and was now swallowing liberal portions of whiskey from the full bottle he'd brought along to ease the stress.

A few minutes earlier she had heard riders pound out of town. She guessed the posse, which Wyatt Earp had led forth in search of the four men who had made the attempt on the stage, was on its way.

It dawned on Kate then what it was that bothered

Doc; his idol, Deputy U. S. Marshal Wyatt Earp, had not chosen him to be a member of the party. She felt a small triumph at the realization. The lawman would one day turn upon him, she'd told Doc many times; now it seemed that it had come to pass. Blunt, as was her nature in such moments, she looked across the room at him and smiled.

"Know why he didn't want you in that posse? Just don't trust you, Doc."

Holliday took another drink and stirred angrily. "Oh, shut your goddamn mouth!" he snarled.

"Always said he wasn't the friend you claimed. Only wanted to use you and your gun when the job was too big for him alone."

"I've ridden posse with him before. This one's different."

"Different? How?"

"Looks like Bill Leonard was one of the bunch that stopped the stage and shot the driver and a passenger."

Leonard—the man who owned a jewelry store in Las Vegas, and who'd warned Doc that day when the Law and Order Committee was after him. She had seen him in town once or twice, just supposed he was visiting.

"They sure of that?"

"Seem to be."

Kate settled back. "Shows how much faith Earp puts in you. Leonard's your friend, figures if it came down to arresting him you'd be against it."

"Wyatt knows I always pay my debts and I owe Bill a favor. Didn't want to embarrass me."

"Sure, sure. Who'd he take along?"

172

"Morgan and Virgil. Fellow by the name of Williams, Bat Masterson and the shotgun rider that was on the stage, Bob Paul. Your friend Behan went too, him and his deputy, Breakenridge."

"The sheriff's no particular friend of mine," Kate retorted. "I thought he and Earp didn't get along."

"They don't. Behan's just looking to get the job done for him. Probably hasn't got the backbone to take on those four who stopped the stage. His out is that since there was U.S. mail on the coach, it's government business and that lays it on Wyatt."

"You think they'll catch the holdup men?"

"Doubt it. Expect they'll duck over the border into Mexico, and that'll end it."

She could wish that Earp would cross the line and get lost forever, but no such good luck would come her way. The lawman would be back, with or without the outlaws, riding down Fremont in that proud, arrogant way, and Doc would go trotting after him to kiss his boots, as always.

Regardless of excuses, he'd been hurt by Earp's refusal to let him ride with the posse. She could tell by the way he spoke, and by his actions. And being hurt, he'd come to her, she realized suddenly. He'd needed to talk about it and she had been his choice. It stirred a ray of hope within her.

"Notice John Ringo hanging around you every time he comes to town."

Kate's brows came up. "So? He's a friend and a gentleman—"

"Gentleman!" Doc echoed with a scornful laugh. "He doesn't know the meaning of the word."

She'd forgotten about that first day when they'd

173

encountered Ringo and Doc's reaction to the man. "It makes a difference to you—him and me, I mean?"

"Hell, no. Just figure you could do better. One of these days I'll probably have to kill him."

Abruptly he came to his feet. "You doing all right?"

Kate nodded. There was very little remaining of the five thousand she had when they came to Tombstone. She had learned the hard way that she was not in a class with the professionals where gambling was concerned, but with what she made when she chose to sell her wares, she was comfortable.

"Doing fine. Hear your luck's still good."

"Providence making it easy for a dying man," he said with a twisted grin, and crossing to the door, he stepped out into the hall.

She heard him walk the length of the uncarpeted corridor, and rising and going to the window she watched him turn into the street and head for the Oriental. There was a dull ache within her as she stood there, eyes upon his striding figure. They were as far apart as two persons could be. Once close, they could now sit and talk of matters without a hint of guilt or embarrassment.

She wished now that she'd asked him to stay, had shown more interest. Maybe, with Wyatt Earp not around to claim his attention, they could have hashed things over, mutually apologized for slurs made publicly in haste and patched up their affair. But she had not thought of it in time, probably because she was too proud to beg, and she knew him too well to believe he'd take the first steps toward a reconciliation. Likely any such arrangement would have had no permanency, anyway: Earp would return and their life together would fall apart as before.

Some time later when she was in the Alhambra, a copy of one of the local newspapers was handed her by one of the girls. She pointed to an article in it that claimed that Doc had been a member of the gang that held up the stage and killed the two men.

Kate read it and shrugged it off. He wouldn't have gotten himself involved in something like that, even if there was a lot of money to be had. She listened to the talk that went around. The anti-Earp crowd was making the most of it, since Doc was a close friend of the lawman's. It didn't bother him any, only brought that sardonic look to his features.

"If I'd been there," she heard him say, "you can bet I would've got that eight thousand and not bungled it like they did. All a man had to do was down one of the horses. The rest would have been easy."

Knowing Doc and his expertise, Kate believed that. He would never have made the mess of it that the four holdup men had, but the talk persisted, and after a time she began to wonder.

"You think they'll arrest Doc?" she asked one of the bartenders.

"They'd like to, but they ain't got enough evidence to prove anything. I figure it's just Sheriff Behan and his gang trying to trump up something that'll hurt Wyatt and get Doc out of the way. Hell, they're even trying to say that the Earps were in on it now!"

Kate guessed that was probably the truth of it and let it slide from her mind, taking only small note of the posse's empty-handed return some days later.

The even tenor of her life resumed. She saw Doc almost every evening at one or another of the saloons but he paid no more visits to their rooms, and finally, in the interests of convenience and economy, she moved from the hotel to one of the cabins south of Sixth Street.

It was a narrow world in which she now existed, and little of what was happening on Fremont or Allen streets reached her attention until it was news out of the past, and therefore of small interest. She did learn that three of the men pursued by the Earp posse for the Benson stage holdup and killings had been slain in another attempt. The fourth had been caught, she seemed to recall, but had escaped.

Doc would be feeling down over Leonard's death. Bill had done him a favor and he'd not had the opportunity to pay him back, and that was something he made a point of doing, returning a kindness or an injury. It was a religion with him.

23

Kate was furious. Holliday had humiliated her several times in the past months but this was the worst of all—telling that gambler friend of his that she was old, that she was worn out, and that he personally wouldn't touch her with ten-foot pole.

Well, by God, she was still one hell of a lot of woman, if she did have to say so herself! Doc was just jealous of her, of how she was able to get along fine without him, and it griped him plenty that she had some mighty big friends, like Johnny Ringo and Curly Bill and the superintendent of the Blue Bell mine, and some other important men.

Hell, he had no right to talk about her the way he was, she thought as she sat, that July day, at a back table in a saloon on Allen Street. It wasn't right. Maybe she had said some mean things about him but never anything that was real mean.

"He hadn't ought've done that to me," she muttered thickly, pouring herself another drink. "Just ain't right."

Somewhere around dark, when she could neither tell nor care whether it was day or night, old friend Mike Joyce with Sheriff Johnny Behan appeared and sat down at her table, each bringing as a gift a full quart bottle of whiskey.

Kate considered them both through a wavering haze and wagged her head loosely. "Some other time, boys."

Joyce laughed and shoved his liquid offering toward her. "Not what we're here for, Kate."

She grasped Joyce's bottle, reached for Behan's bottle and gathered them to her. "What for then?"

"Nothing special. Saw you sitting here moping over that bastard of a Doc Holliday. He shouldn't be treating you the way he is."

"That son of a bitch," she agreed dully.

"That talking he's doing about you," Behan put in, "no decent man'd ever do that to a woman."

"Not after all the things you've done for him!" Joyce added.

Kate nodded sluggishly. Here were two people who understood all she'd been through for Doc. "Done a plenty, can tell you that for sure."

"No doubt about it," Behan said. "All those scrapes he got into and you had to pull him out of and then turning against you like he has—it ain't right."

"The truth!" Kate declared loudly. "If it hadn't been for me back there in The Flat they'd a-lynched him for killing Ed Bailey."

"That so?" Joyce said, refilling her glass. "Can you recollect any other times like that?"

"Plenty. Was that jasper up in Las Vegas he shot. Expect the law's still wanting him for that. Was me that kept the vigilantes standing in my bedroom while

178

he got away. Then there's that holdup charge in Dodge. Told the marshal he was with me when it happened.

"Some others he just told me about—a cowhand he killed in Cheyenne, a miner he knifed during a fight in Tiger Alley up in Leadville. Down in Texas he's wanted for killings in Dallas and Jonesboro and somewheres else. Same for Trinidad and, it seems, La Junta, up in Colorado."

"No different here in Tombstone," Behan said. "There was those two fellows he was gambling with that he shot down in cold blood just because they complained about not being able to win once in a while. For my money Doc Holliday is a crook and a sneak and we sure shouldn't let him get away with things the way he does—especially talking about you."

Kate, befuddled and besotted, struggled to focus her eyes on the two men. They were taking up for her against Doc, she decided. They agreed with her that he had not treated her right.

"It's about time somebody straightened him out," Joyce said firmly. "I think the whole town ought to know about him, about how he's treated you, and we're going to help you do that."

"Do what?" Kate wondered, helping herself unsteadily to another drink.

"Tell folks just how low down and mean Holliday is—that is unless you're afraid."

"I ain't afraid of him—"

"That's good," Behan said, taking a paper from his pocket and unfolding it on the table before her. "You sign this and we'll make Doc take back everything he's said about you."

Kate pawed at the sheet and frowning, attempted to read the words written upon it. "What's this?"

"It's a paper telling about all the things you did for Holliday and how he then turned against you and made you look bad to all your friends—just what you got through telling us, Kate."

"We're going to print it in the newspaper. That way everybody'll know the truth," Joyce said. "Here's a pencil."

She stared at the sheet before her. In her whiskey-soaked state of mind it never occurred to her to question how it happened that Behan and Joyce could have compiled such a list of the incidents related to them before they'd even talked to her. She was conscious only of a strong indignation and a need to get even with Doc.

Taking the pencil, she signed the paper. Behan grinned broadly, scooped it up, folded it, and tucked it back inside his coat pocket.

"Want you to know, Kate, you've done the right thing," he said in a loud voice as he got to his feet.

Joyce, also rising, leaned over to her. "Doc Holliday's going to be sorry he ever treated you like dirt," he said.

Kate bobbed and poured herself another portion of liquor. "I'll show him," she muttered. "Never did appreciate me like he ought."

Kate glanced up for confirmation. Behan and Joyce were gone. She shrugged. It didn't matter. They'd left her the two quarts of whiskey, and now were on their way to the newspaper with the story that would straighten folks out about her and Doc. Who knows, it might even sort of jar Doc a little, make him realize what he'd done and bring him back to her?

One of the girls came over and sat down opposite her at the table. Flushed at what she may have accomplished, Kate invited her to have a drink. The girl, Mitzi, pulled the cork of one of the full bottles and took a swallow.

"What did those two highbinders want?" she asked, studying Kate suspiciously.

"They're helping me to bring Doc to time," she explained. "He's going to find out it's not right to throw me over, then go talking about me."

Mitzi gave that thought and shook her head. "You better go home, Kate. I've got a feeling you'd best get out of sight."

"Me—what for?"

"Behan hates Doc. You know that. Hates him because he's a good friend of Wyatt Earp's. If you've done something to help Behan and his bunch—"

"All I've done was tell them about Doc, how he treated me and talked about me after all I went through for him."

"What was that paper you signed?"

"Just what I said. Told about him and me and how I helped him. They're going to print it in the newspaper so's everybody'll know."

Mitzi shrugged. "Don't make sense to me, but one thing sure, you're too drunk to be signing your name to something."

"I know what I'm doing!" Kate shouted, suddenly belligerent. "You're taking up for Doc! Well, go ahead, see if I care. He's going to learn he can't do things like that to me."

Mitzi listened in silence, shrugged again and walked off toward the bar.

Kate continued to sit at the table, drinking steadily.

181

The swamper appeared and lit the rest of the oil lamps, the crowd began to increase and soon the night's business got under way. Mitzi, in company with another of the girls, Hortense, stopped by. Both encouraged her to go home, lock the door and sleep off the effects of all the whiskey she had consumed.

Morose and sullen, Kate stubbornly refused. "Going to wait right here," she mumbled.

"Wait—for who?"

"For—for Doc! Soon as he hears about the newspaper he's going to come find me, say he's sorry."

Had she been able to think only passably clearly, Kate would have known that was impossible. Holliday never apologized to anyone regardless of the situation. But the quantity of liquor sloshing her brain dulled her senses to the point of imbecility.

A man pushed through the dimness and stood before her at the table. She leaned forward eagerly.

"Doc?"

"It's not Doc," Mitzi said kindly. "It's Marshal Earp."

Kate jerked back angrily. "Wyatt Earp. What the hell's he doing here? I won't talk to him. He's the reason me and Doc—"

"Not Wyatt, Virgil," Mitzi broke in. "The town marshal."

"Glad I finally found you, Kate," the lawman said in a relieved voice. "I'm locking you up."

"Why?" Hortense demanded, bristling.

"Holliday's out to kill her," Earp replied.

24

Kate stirred feebly. "What'd he say?"

Mitzi, glancing at Hortense, turned to Earp. "This got something to do with that paper she signed for Sheriff Behan?"

The marshal, his features stiff and unyielding, nodded. "That paper was an affidavit naming Doc Holliday as one of the outlaws that held up the Benson stage and murdered two men."

The woman swore deeply. "I knew it! Just had to be something crooked in what they were doing."

Earp's expression did not change. "She swore Doc was in on it. He's been arrested."

Kate slumped in her chair, head bowed. She was conscious only of the sound of words, not of their meaning. Mitzi reached out, laid a hand on her shoulder and shook her violently.

"You understand what he's saying? Doc's been arrested and put in jail. That paper you signed for the sheriff put him there—"

"Not in jail now," Earp broke in. "Judge Spicer

183

let him out on bond. Wyatt and a couple other men signed for him. He's free and walking the street. That's why I'm here. Want to get her locked up safe in jail before he finds her."

Mitzi threw a nervous glance toward the doorway. "She be all right there?"

"I'll see to it. She's no good to us dead. We've got it figured that it's all a frame-up by Behan. We know Holliday had nothing to do with the Benson stage. Behan and Joyce just saw a chance to get at Wyatt through Doc by getting Kate drunk and talking her into signing an affidavit accusing him."

"She thinks it was just a paper telling how Doc had treated her mean."

Virgil Earp considered Kate enigmatically. "Can believe that. Condition she's in she'd believe anything they told her."

"Once she sobers up and realizes what she's done, you can bet she'll straighten it all out."

"That's what Wyatt thinks. Wants her locked up tight where Doc can't get to her and where she can't get any more liquor. Then when Holliday goes before the judge she can testify that she didn't know what she was signing, and that what's on the affidavit is a lie."

Earp, moving around behind the table, put his hands under Kate's arms, drew her upright and glanced about.

"Just hoping I can make it to the jail with her without running into Holliday," he said tautly. "He's really up in the air. Keeps saying that nothing riles him more than to have a friend sell him out to an enemy."

Mitzi sniffed, drew her lips into a scornful smile.

184

"Friend! He sure was no friend of hers! If he was, then she sure don't need any enemies!"

"Don't know about that," Earp murmured, waving aside the small crowd that had quietly gathered to listen. He started for the back door of the saloon. "Just know I've got to sober her up and keep her alive so's she can tell a straight story. Otherwise Behan's got Holliday nailed to the cross."

"Maybe that ain't such a bad idea."

A ghost of a smile crossed Earp's face. "All a matter of opinion, I suspect," he said. "Anyway, it's Wyatt I'm looking out for."

It was over quickly. Kate, restricted to the confines of a cell in the Tombstone jail, and under the constant protection of the town marshal and his deputy, came to her senses and to a realization of what she had been tricked into doing.

Now, subdued and standing before Judge Spicer, she listened to the charges made against Doc in the affidavit. The courtroom was crowded, and Holliday, sitting at the same table as she but at its opposite end, coughed occasionally. She had carefully avoided his glance throughout the proceedings.

"Yes, sir, I did," she answered when the court exhibited the affidavit and asked if she had signed it.

"Is the deposition thereon true?"

"No, sir, it's not. I didn't know what I was signing. I don't know anything about the Benson stage holdup."

"Then why did you sign such a statement?"

"They told me—"

"Who told you?"

"Sheriff Behan and Mike Joyce."

"All right, go on."

"I was drinking some, and then they came up to my table. They each brought me a full bottle of whiskey and we started talking about Doc. They said he was mean to be saying the things he was saying about me, after all I'd done for him, and that folks ought to know about it. Then the sheriff brought out that paper and told me to sign it. He said he was going to have it printed in the newspaper."

"What did he say was written on the paper?"

"That it told how Doc treated me mean, and after it was published people would know what kind of a man he was and not believe the things he was saying about me."

"Didn't you read it before you signed it?"

"No. I guess I was real drunk."

"But you believed what Behan and Joyce told you was written on it."

"Yes, sir," Kate said in a low voice. "I was mad at Doc but I wouldn't lie about him. I didn't know anything about that holdup. They just fooled me into saying I did."

Spicer released her at that point and she resumed her place at the table. Other witnesses were called to bear further evidence of Doc Holliday's innocence. Finally it was finished and the charges were dropped.

Kate got to her feet and turned for the door. Her friends, Mitzi and Hortense, among the spectators, rose to go with her, and together they stepped out into the hot July sunshine.

A hand caught at Kate's shoulder and pulled her roughly about. It was Doc, anger tearing at his lean features. At one side of him stood her old enemy, Wyatt Earp, at the other, Virgil. Holliday started to

186

speak, oaths crackling from his lips, and then a fit of coughing stilled the words.

Wyatt Earp stepped in front of him. "Your life's not worth a plugged nickel around here," he said. "I want you out of town on the next stage." Reaching into his inside coat pocket, he produced a roll of currency and handed it to her. "There's a thousand dollars here. Take it and get as far from Tombstone as you can—and don't ever come back."

Kate accepted the money and was silent for a long moment. Then, "This from you?"

"All of us—Doc included. We raised it among us," Earp said. "Stage leaves in an hour. Be on it."

Kate turned away, and with Hortense and Mitzi headed slowly for her lodgings. Reaching the corner she paused and looked back. Doc had recovered from his seige of coughing, and like the Earps, was watching her move off.

"We'll miss you," Mitzi said. "A shame you have to go."

"I won't miss Tombstone," Kate snapped, some of the old fire returning as she continued on. "And I sure as hell won't miss any of them!"

But she knew she would—at least one of them. They'd had good times together, she and Doc, and there'd be no forgetting him, not if she lived a hundred years. It was ending now, however; she'd betrayed him to his enemies, all unawares to be sure, but she had, nevertheless, and she neither asked for nor expected his forgiveness. It was the finish, and strong woman that she was, she accepted it without a whimper.

AUTHOR'S NOTE

Since she had no dedicated biographer to faithfully log the events crowding her turbulent years, this story of Big Nose Kate Elder (or Fisher) was of necessity pieced together by bits and scraps, with logic and speculation playing a major role in its compilation. Therefore this book should primarily be considered fiction with references being made to persons real, places existent and dates approximate.

Grateful acknowledgment is made herein to the following authors and their works for certain background information:

Stuart Lake: WYATT EARP, FRONTIER LAW-MAN Houghton-Mifflin Boston 1931

Dee Brown & Martin F. Smith: TRAIL DRIVING DAYS Bonanza Books New York 1952

Douglas D. Martin: TOMBSTONE'S EPITAPH Univ. of New Mexico Press Albuquerque 1951

John Myers Myers: DOC HOLLIDAY
  Little, Brown & Co.   New York   1955
Carl W. Breihan: GREAT LAWMEN OF THE
  WEST Bonanza Books   New York   1963
Walter Noble Burns: TOMBSTONE
  Doubleday & Co.   New York   1927
Stanley Vestal: DODGE CITY, QUEEN OF COW-
  TOWNS Harper Bros.   New York   1952
William Waters: WESTERN BADMEN
  Americana Publications   Covington, Ken.   1954

Ray Hogan is an author who has inspired a loyal following over the years since he published his first Western novel *Ex-Marshal* in 1956. Hogan was born in Willow Springs, Missouri, where his father was town marshal. At five the Hogan family moved to Albuquerque where Ray Hogan still lives in the foothills of the Sandia and Manzano mountains. His father was on the Albuquerque police force and, in later years, owned the Overland Hotel. It was while listening to his father and other old-timers tell tales from the past that Ray was inspired to recast these tales in fiction. From the beginning he did exhaustive research into the history and the people of the Old West and the walls of his study are lined with various firearms, spurs, pictures, books, and memorabilia, about all of which he can talk in dramatic detail. Among his most popular works are the series of books about Shawn Starbuck, a searcher in quest for a lost brother who has a clear sense of right and wrong and who is willing to stand up and be counted when it is a question of fairness or justice. His other major series is about lawman John Rye whose reputation has earned him the sobriquet The Doomsday Marshal. 'I've attempted to capture the courage and bravery of those men and women that lived out West and the dangers and problems they had to overcome,' Hogan once remarked. If his lawmen protagonists seem sometimes larger than life, it is because they are men of integrity, heroes who through grit of character and common sense are able to overcome the obstacles they encounter despite often overwhelming odds. This same grit of character can also be found in Hogan's heroines and in *The Vengeance of Fortuna West* Hogan wrote a gripping and totally believable account of a woman who takes up the badge and tracks the men who killed her lawman husband by ambush. No less intriguing in her way is Nellie Dupray, convicted of rustling in *The Glory Trail*. Above all, what is most impressive about Hogan's Western novels is the consistent quality with which each is crafted, the compelling depth of his characters, and his ability to juxtapose the complexities of human conflict into narratives always as intensely interesting as they are emotionally involving.